The Damnation
of Vancouver

Earle Birney

A New Canadian Library Selection
With an Introduction by Wai Lan Low

GENERAL EDITOR: Malcolm Ross

A New Canadian Library Original No. o11

McClelland and Stewart

ISBN 0-7710-9515-5

The original radio version of the play (one-and-a-half hours) was performed on the Transcanada network of the Canadian Broadcasting Corporation, October 8, 1952. A full text of this version appears in the author's *Trial of a City and Other Verse*, Ryerson Press, Toronto, 1952. Two public readings of this version were given at the University of British Columbia, the first constituting the formal opening of the Frederic Wood Theatre, December 6, 1952, the second at a special presentation of the U.B.C. Player's Club in the university auditorium in 1954.

The present version constitutes a complete revision and adaptation for the stage, and was first presented by a group of University of British Columbia players at the University of Washington, Seattle, February 10, 1957. A public reading of this stage version was given by members of the drama department of the Universidad Nacionale de México in Mexico City, September, 1962.

The Canadian Publishers
McClelland and Stewart Limited
25 Hollinger Road
Toronto, Ontario

Printed in Canada By Webcom Limited

Preface

Twenty-five years ago, in the great Age of Radio, when people listened to the words, the evening news from Victoria told me that the B.C. government had begun a week's Public Hearing in the town of Courtenay to consider arguments for and against its proposal to dam Buttle Lake. Courtenay was only a few miles from the cottage I'd rented in the woods of central Vancouver Island, and I drove there the next morning. I was curious what a Public Hearing was like, but I was also concerned. Buttle, despite its drab name, was an environmental symbol: the last unspoiled glacier lake in all the fourteen thousand square miles of the Island. It lay in the heart of Strathcona Park, a game and forest preserve, home of the last of the island bighorns, a wilderness approachable only by trail or float-plane. Away back in 1868 another government had the vision to set aside this park "in perpetuity". Could there be any possible reason for disrupting it in 1951?

Reasons of a sort were resounding at the Hearing in the little town hall. Precedent was one of them. A dam had been built up, 142 feet high and a half-mile wide, six years before, beside the Park's boundary, ruining the looks and the fishing of a nearby lake and obliterating Elk Falls, the Island's loveliest. Huge pipes had already been run from this dam down a wild canyon to a hydroelectric plant, and the inevitable power lines slashed through firs and orchards all the way to Victoria. Two years ago a second dam had been added to the system, flooding another lake. The newest plan was simply to add yet another pair of dams, eliminating another fine waterfall, and Buttle Lake. Why? Because industry needed more power, to grow more industry. That was the basic reason: industry was progress and progress had a higher price tag than beauty.

There were objectors. People whose property would be flooded, some of them, walked up to the front of the hall and actually said they preferred to go on running their fishing lodges or tourist inns rather than take compensation in cash and retire to the town. And there was the owner of a local logging outfit who was concerned about the plan to cut down one of the last stands of original Douglas Fir, all around Buttle Lake, before raising the lake level; but his concern was only that the government, he suspected, had already let the contract to one of the big companies. He was later proved right, as was the statistically-minded engineer who had a brief to show that the proposed development, though laudable, would satisfy the demands of industry for only another five years, after which power would have to be brought under or over the sea from the mainland.

Yet, apart from the writer Roderick Haig-Brown, none at the Hearing seemed really to feel alarmed by this endless vista of urban expansion into their green island. One weekend fisherman was delighted that roads would now be pushed into Buttle Lake; it always took too long to hike in over the trail, and he couldn't afford to own a seaplane like these American millionaires. A local merchant and Nimrod felt it was more people we needed, not bighorns you weren't allowed to shoot anyway. A middle-aged lady hoped that opening up the Park would put an end to those cougars that preyed on schoolchildren.

I drove back through acrid smoke to our parched lawn, now flecked with ash. This evening's radio reported the latest forest fire was burning out of control, from a logging operation. I started to scribble something. The Hearing had given me not only the emotional need to write, but the form: an odd sort of trial-drama, more relaxed, less cliché-ridden than a court of law; witnesses need not be sworn; they simply expressed opinions. A play of ideas about dammings, about the ultimate damning.

By next spring I had a two-hour radio drama, *The Damnation of Vancouver*. Accepted, trimmed by a half-hour, it was given a stirring production by Andrew Allen for the opening of his autumn Stage series over the Transcanda network of the CBC. Although ignored by the reviewers in the Toronto papers, the telephone calls, telegrams and letters I got told me it had been a radio success. A lot of people, including even the Vancouver Tourist Bureau, wanted to read the script, if only to damn it. I was encouraged to make the play the title-piece of a new book of poems which were contracted to the Ryerson Press. Ryersons, however, for reasons explicable only to United Churchmen, refused at the last moment to accept 'damnation'. The word was O.K. in the text, but too shocking on the cover. They substituted "Trial of a City". Whether despite the emasculated title, or because of it, the book went into three printings and by 1954 was being studied in a course at the University of Alberta.

It had also been given two public readings at the University of British Columbia. The first was by the Graduate Players Club at the formal opening of the original Frederic Wood Theatre in 1952. The second, a "dress reading" with masks, was presented by undergraduates of the Club in 1954. It was visually successful enough to reawaken CBC interest in the play. By 1956 I had been commissioned to re-cast it as a one-hour drama for television. This was accepted, paid for, and scheduled for "early 1957". For reasons the CBC never divulged to me, it was never produced. The rumour was it had been one of several scheduled plays shelved that year to appease a parliamentary committee investigating "highbrowism" in CBC programming.

Meantime, having this new visual "Damnation" on my hands, I decided to reshape it once more, this time, into a stage play. No theatre in Vancouver wanted it, but in February, 1957, a group of UBC players was invited to Seattle to present Vancouver's damnation, from mimeographed scripts, in the University of Washington's theatre. Later, Tyrone Guthrie read one of these scripts, considering it for Stratford, Ont. He thought it would need a major revision to make it suitable for the professional theatre, but was warm in his praise of its readability, and urged me to have it published.

In 1958 the opportunity came at last for both publication and professional performance. The B.C. government declared a Centennial and appointed committees to arrange celebrations. The cultural sub-committee of the Vancouver Committee actually recommended a full-scale production of my stage *Damnation* for the ten days. It was to provide the chief open-air entertainment at the reconstructed Fort Langley, and its first night would be presided over by Princess Margaret.

But then the chairman of the main Centennial Committee read the play. He was a very devout alderman, clubman, chain-store merchant and landowner. It is possible, though he never said so, that he saw his spiritual brother maligned as Mr. Legion. What he did say was that Gassy Jack would have to be dematerialized even before the play started, and replaced by Centennial Sam. The latter was a cartoon line-drawing of a winsome old prospector, used on Centennial promotional material. I was requested to write Jack out and Sam in. When I refused I lost my last chance, it seems, to watch my play on Canadian boards.

I did, however, have the fun of playing the part of Gabriel

5

Powers in a second reading production of the present version in September 1962; the other players were members of the Drama Department of the Universidad Nacional de México. Perhaps if I had written a Damnation of Mexico City or of Seattle or Edmonton, I would have got it produced in Vancouver. Meanwhile I am very grateful that my publishers in Toronto have now made it possible for Vancouverites and other Canadians to read this final version of the *Damnation of Vancouver*, in print here for the first time.

September 1976

Earle Birney

Introduction

The incident which provided the source for *The Damnation of Vancouver* was, as the author has told us, a public hearing on the proposed damming of Buttle Lake in Strathcona Park, Vancouver Island, in 1951. The proposal, made by provincial politicians and industrial magnates to secure cheap power and timber, had the inevitable result of destroying the only unspoiled glacial lake remaining on Vancouver Island. Because the issue coincided with the depths of the cold war and the mounting threat of atomic annihilation, it led Birney to pose two questions: first, since our civilization willingly and knowingly lays waste the very earth and air that support it, will it not with equal knowledge and willingness proceed to destroy man himself? And, more importantly, is man worth saving from his own destructive irresponsibility? From the moment of Hiroshima, the Shavian proposition that the human species will be discarded if it does not "come up to the mark" has continued to be the dominant fear of thinking man. Humanity had now achieved the technology to make the ultimate judgement, and remove not only our own civilization but all life from the face of the earth.

The city, and the city of Vancouver in particular, becomes in this play the medium through which Birney considers the totality of man's accomplishments and failures. His trial is of a whole culture, of modern man. Vancouver, though presented with intimate social and geographical detail, is Everycity– an aggregate of urban life and feeling, an emblem of the dubiously "best" achievements of our civilization. The characters who preside over and testify at the public hearing are archetypes or allegorical personifications of processes, and the hearing, though taking the shape of a futuristic fantasy, really belongs to the genre of the morality play, a form which, by its expository and allegorical nature, allows Birney to transform his meditation on mankind's hope for salvation or looming damnation into a dialectic. Hence we are given the city through telling rather than through showing, and the telling in this case is a method oddly more direct and more revealing of Birney's own ambivalent attitudes about the civilization the city represents.

Like Bernard Shaw, one of his chief dramatic and philosophical influences, Birney speaks through his characters but his world vision is too complex to be lodged in any single one of them. What results is an argument made possible by fragmenting his cautious, complex, questioning vision of the city into a number of relatively simple and unambivalent points of view—though the vision as a whole is much greater than any summation of its parts. The versification, which varies from fourteenth-century alliteration by the ghost of Langland to the Joycean double-talk of Gabriel Powers, serves to emphasize the historical perspective in which Birney is trying to view Vancouver and the life it represents. By the means of ghosts materialized out of Vancouver's past, the city's time is telescoped, and what is established metaphorically is the concept that all of a city's past, all of its ghosts *are* in the present: they have created what is now, and remain, waiting to be recreated in spirit or in act. But just as the risen dead are the spirit of the city's past, so the living characters of the play are a distillation of the city's present. It is what they are as by-products of the city, and what they reveal of the urban culture in their attempts to defend Vancouver, that ironically damns the city rather than saves it. Even Mrs. Anyone, who reaffirms faith in the individual quest for life and in the power of love, does not redeem the urban system; she cannot deny the evils of the city, only transcend them. The play posits a basis of hope for mankind's future, but it does not resolve the two basic questions as they apply to the actual city of Vancouver or, presumably, to any other city.

Birney is something of an ideologue: while admitting the inevitability of community as part of human life, he also constructs an inclusive theory uniting the city with the machine, with commerce, with arid rationality and calculation, with outrage against the land, and with a preponderance of inhuman values that destroy deep community spirit and man's inner harmony. Birney's Vancouver is a city to be distrusted if not feared. Though the temporal relationship between the total history of Vancouver as city and the date of this play is similar to that between the total history of New York or Boston and the date of criticisms aimed at those cities by Emerson, Hawthorne or James, there is in Birney's work no sense of a lost agrarian or pastoral ideal to provide an alternative. There is only an elegiac regret for the dying cultures of the Indian and for the intenser life of the pioneer, and an exhortation to modern man to live in a way that is more sane, and more ecologically sound than his present habits and values permit. This is perhaps attributable to the aim of the play to be concerned chiefly with the salvageability of mankind as a whole. Yet the other fact remains that the work does specifically identify the urban artifact with corruption, vulgarity, and sterility, with the breakdown of tribal ties and social values, and with artificial and rather meaningless measurement, all related to a culture foolishly obsessed with ever-increasing productivity and the reckless cannibalization of the environment. For Birney, the debilities imposed on the individual by the city are not an unfortunate result of a sound civilization (as they were for Jefferson)—they are the sad result of a culture whose values could not bear grave scrutiny.

The hearing is set significantly in a small hall in the basement of the Vancouver Court House—one of the follies of our culture is that it is likely to give far less attention to the crucial problems than to the trivial. The hearing on the damning of Buttle Lake was in fact held in a basement room of the town hall in the small town of Courtenay, B.C., during work hours, and was attended by few. When the proposed damnation of Vancouver is aired, it seems that only a few hired witnesses are available, and only one free citizen presents herself for the city's defence. The average inhabitant is too complacent and self-insulated to get involved with the world beyond the immediately familiar and structured environment of home, work,—and leisure for television.

> President: You wouldn't expect a Vancouverite to
> come all the way down in the rain to
> this Court House cellar when any chair
> at home is softer?

Vancouver has a champion, however, in Legion, a conventional pillar of the community, an emblem of the city's best, an orthodox believer in Vancouver's present "success" and future "progress". He symbolizes the mass ethos, the public pride in the city's collective mercantile and industrial achievements and, like Voltaire's Doctor Pangloss, understands nothing but the material present, even if that. His paraphernalia are tourist pamphlets, law books, and the city directory—he is the archetypal corporation/public man, drugged by statistics, by propaganda, by pecuniary measurement. If Legion is the true symbol of the spokesman for the city, and if the city is to be judged for what it is now, it is spiritually doomed, for Legion is myopic, dull and totally unreflecting in his acceptance of the most conventional and impersonal values. He is the Majority, as his name denotes, and he is blind to any of the important human problems and hopes that generate life and change. *Sub species aeternitas*, he is as much a multiple madman and devil as his Biblical namesake (Mark V, 9).

The two other major figures among the hearing officials, the presiding Minister of History and Gabriel Powers, the counsel for the Office of the Future, are more purely allegorical both in character and in function in the play. The Minister of History is the cold objective judgement of mankind in hindsight—hence only the dead are to him proper witnesses to man's achievements or failures. Powers is the principle of justice as man creates it for himself through action—he is an oracle representing fate as well as a projection of man's own sense of guilt and fear of death. The hearing, therefore, is the sort of outrageous kangaroo court that was probably typical of the congressional committees of the McCarthy era, and the city is doomed to annihilation unless it can prove itself worth saving. A weighty challenge.

Episode 2 begins the demonstration of the city's failing vitality and misguided values as the explorer Captain George Vancouver is materialized to give his opinion of the present condition of the city whose site he discovered. Legion's argument for the city's preservation on the basis of its size, its rapid growth from virgin wilderness to metropolis, and its fancy university ("totem poles, tetanus farms,/Canned TV lectures, rocket alarms—/Bigger than Oxford . . . ") fails to impress Captain Vancouver. Having witnessed both the raw landscape as he found it in the eighteenth century and the city that eventually resulted, he concludes that the latter is little improvement and he voices Birney's distaste for the machine's and industry's destructive infringement on the land:

> I'll wager Burrard's proud to know his harbour
> Is toothed with docks from lar-to-star-board;
> But all this town—these gross mechanic jaws
> That clamp and champ around the sea—

Ultimately, even the overly celebrated fact of its having been hacked from the timber in three generations has brought disadvantage to the city because the very expansion which made it a metropolis in such a phenomenally short time also created a city without tradition. The final and most deflating blow that Captain Vancouver inflicts on Legion's pride in Vancouver's crassness is to decide that it does not measure up to eighteenth century London, and so is a superfluity:

A feat indeed in such a trifling time
To piece together so much wood and grime;
'Tis huge as my old Lunnon, and as dun,
As planless, not so plaguey—but less fun.
I rather liked the sweep of fir and cedar.
Your city? Sir, I can't think why we need her.

Next the Salish Headman, Skuh-wath-kwuh-lath-kyootl, materializes to compare the kind of life which existed on Burrard Inlet when Captain Vancouver arrived with the present culture of Vancouver. The Salish Headman is too extraordinarily and perhaps unjustifiably eloquent and persuasive in presenting his own culture as superior to that of the white man, but the subjects of this section of the play are the city's lack of harmony and integrity in the relationships between man and man and between man and the environment, and the city's lack of a traditional life. As the Chief says:

Where once we hunted, white men have built many
    longhouses,
But they move uneasy as mice within them.
They have made slaves from waterfalls
And magic from the souls of rocks.
They are stronger than grizzlies.
But their slaves bully them,
And they are chickadees in council.
Some of you say (Turning towards Legion.) "Give us time,
We will grow wise, and invent peace."
(Turning to Powers)
Others say: "The sun slides into the saltchuck;
We must follow the Redman into the trail of darkness."

The Indian had the stability of a strong communal life and a continuing interdependence with nature which, though it may not have produced enough to satisfy the profit motive, always provided enough. As the Headman points out, "It was not till

11

your time, sir (Turning to Legion)/I saw a Salish go hungry." Though the modern Vancouverite has the security of bureaucratic government, codified laws, and the belief that his civilization is the culmination of thousands of years of "thinking", he also has the sterility of urban solipsism and alienation from the land. He has lost sight of the simple arts and pleasures—he may have aluminum pressure cookers, but, as the Headman notes, "it does not have our wave pattern." He may have abundant goods of all sorts but not the Indian's tradition of proud and joyful giving, formalized in the potlatch. And finally, he has not the Indian's fully sensual, vital intimacy with nature that is not the result of any conceptualized ideal of relationship with the earth but rather of experience and discovery:

> Chief: Sometimes a young man would be many months thinking,
> Alone in the woods as a heron,
> And learning the Powers of the creatures.
> When I was young I lay and watched the little grey doctor,
> The lizard, I studied his spirit, I found his song,
> When I was Chief (With a touch of pride.) I carved him on my house-posts.
> I took the red earths and the white, and painted his wisdom.

Legion, who has the modern city man's distrust of knowledge which cannot be considered scientific, dismisses the Chief's intuitional insight into his environment as mere superstition. Legion's world is, formally at any rate, one which values calculation rather than feeling, and which believes in rapid change and "advance" rather than holding to traditional ways and values.

From the Indian's view, Legion's civilization has simply raped the land for the purposes of commercial exploitation, disrupted the Salish harmony with nature, and engulfed his whole race:

> Chief: There was more, a something—I do not know—
> A way of life that died for yours to live.
> We gambled with sticks, and storms, and wives, but we did not steal.
> The Chief my father spoke to the people only what was true.

When there was quarrel, he made us unravel it
with reason,
Or wrestle weaponless on the clean sand.
We kept no longhouses for warriors, we set no
state over others.
Each had his work, and all made certain each was
fed.
It was a way—

Yet while the tone with which Birney treats the way of the
Indian displays sorrow that the native culture had to be de-
stroyed by the city's growth and the white man's civilization,
there is none of the desire to retreat into the past, to retrace or
recreate the earlier way. The failures and crimes of the city
culture are strongly established, but if Vancouver is to be
damned, it must be judged on its own terms, on the degree to
which the urban system can fulfill human needs and hopes. It is
not really fruitful to compare it with a radically different type of
organism, which cannot now be recreated; the last word is not
the Headman's.

In Episode 4 Birney presents not human and subjective attitudes toward the city, as in the other sections of the play, but
rather places the phenomenon of life, man, and civilization into
the perspective of the universe's time and space. The Anglo-
Saxon verse form of Professor E. O. Seen suggests that mankind
is still at some quite primitive stage of development while the
history of the earth he gives reiterates the specialness and fragil-
ity of any kind of life in relation to the violent forces which keep
the universe in flux. The maturation and death of the sun will
likely destroy human life and human artifacts soon enough:

Powers: (Rising, to Seen) Man-Cain this brief new morn-
ing came—
But when a-wither, when away?
O sage Promessor, say.
Seen: (Caught offguard by the question, but remaining
honest scientist.)
Hmmm. Mayhap another thousand generations
till
Ice-press return again, tombing the Inlet.
Legion: Now, now, perffessor, that's only speculation.
Anyway, we'd blast the ice back. Atomic energy.

13

Seen:	Doubtless man can endure, yet this inlet would drown.
Powers:	Forever endure?
Seen:	(Cautiously) Forever? Forever is—long. All suns wane, or swell.
Powers:	And when our sun alters?
Seen:	Then a sleek ball of ice, or of stone boiling.
Powers:	(Relentlessly) And Life?
Seen:	Life? Though man leap to Mars, he is lost in this fury.
Powers:	(Ironic gesture to Hearing.) You hear, O Hearing? To blow this vain Man-cover skywards now is to advanquish by a jingle comic second what Adamizing Father Sun desires. Thank you, Prophetic-facer Sane.

Like the Headman, Gassy Jack, the next witness, gives a glimpse of a more spontaneous and autonomous life out of an irrecoverable past. Jack's undisguised love of the bawdy story, grog, and the ladies is offensive to the more delicate sensibilities of the members of the hearing, but his healthy vice and vulgarity are, as Northrop Frye points out, less sinister than the perversions of the city life of modern Vancouver.[1] Whereas the Headman was emblematic of a culture strongly traditional and in harmony with the earth, Gassy Jack is the embodiment of reckless pioneer vitality and the tough, resilient spirit of individualism creating a new community. Gassy Jack and the other early settlers of Vancouver came to escape and to start afresh, and survived by their own wits; they worked hard yet had fun, and Gastown was small enough to allow a high level of personal involvement. The centre of it all was Gassy Jack's saloon, "hoob of t'port, ... t'loggers opry-house and town the-ayter", and the village forum. In contrast, the city of Vancouver and it present inhabitants seem drained of the vitality that characterized Jack and his two hard-working Klootch-lasses.

In all of Legion's extravagant praises for the city, he never thinks, as Jack does, of individual human beings as creators, never speaks of strong personal commitments or desires; he knows only that Vancouver is a place where money is made—not why. For all of Legion's understanding Vancouver is a place where things exist gratuitously, and where events occur as if of their own volition, a place with buildings and bridges and roads that could have just grown out of the earth. Even Vancouver's debauchery has gone out of focus in the impersonal scale of the city's institutions, as well as by the modern cocktail mix:

> Jack: Eigh, ye've pubs bigger nor icebergs now, lad, but they're as cold to t'spirit, man, and nowt bein droonk but wish-washy cocktails that wouldna get a flea happy, and all like Methody wake wi' nivver a song nor salt-water tale. . . .

Gassy Jack, who has Yorkshire seaport origins, has chosen to be a harbour village man and has acquired the village dweller's distrust of the city. He escaped "a Hull of a place", for the rigors of sea life and later for the "tincan sawmill and a dozen float-shacks." That Vancouver should be so like Hull all over again is to him something akin to a personal betrayal, like the re-christening of the outgrown settlement with the more respectable names of Granville and Vancouver. He associates the city with corruption, predation, and falseness:

> Ye know, mates, there's a desperit pack of hippycrits in big cities—cardsharpers and shipchandlers, and landsharks like what burned up owd Gastown, and psalm-singing sods, preachers like. Ah nivver gi' mooch for most of t' missionary fellers. . . .

Jack suggests a return to his perhaps irrecoverable village ideal as a compromise from annihilation. Whereas Legion wants chiefly to save the artifact of the city, Jack wants to see the preservation of good folk in small settlements.

> Happen there be summat Ahm wantin to say, oney Ah can git me toongue round it—dry as tis. Master Legion here, he's worrit about his city, reet? Aye. But look, now, why all t'fuss? Why worry? Gert bludey ports, why, chaps, they're dime a doozen. When sailorman's yoong, port's nobbut a place for getting drunk and makin loove, and then happen for sailin away from, fast like. And when be he's owd

and fair capped wi' sea, he want nowt but a place
like owd Gastown, place that's small, wi' clean
water around it yet, and gert thoompin trees, and
deer wandering in at night. . . . Coorse, now Ah'm
again destroyin things, even gormless gert cities,
Ah'm agin violence an fights—have ye ivver knowd a
saloon-keeper that wasn't? . . . but leastways ship
out folks we wants to keep, and settle em up
coast, happen, so they'll be starting new places,
little places—and see that we keep em small this
time. Aye, ba goom that's the way.

Yet while Jack as a ghost has the ability to see what has
happened to his village since his lifetime, his judgement remains
limited to that of the nineteenth century pioneer. His proposal is
contrary to the collective mental set of North American culture
to encourage rather than discourage urban growth. Jack's own
experience has been singular and unrepeatable—the frontier era
is over. It is no longer a land of unlimited potential wealth and
opportunity that the hearing is concerned with but rather one
which is and has been abused and wasted and put in danger of
destruction.

Much as Gassy Jack, the Headman, and Captain Vancouver
scorn the city, none have a disdain for it to match that of Long
Will of Langland, the writer who performed the first great English dissection of a city, of London, and who first catalogued
remorselessly the evils that were dooming a society. By intro-
ducing Langland as a witness for the prosecution, Birney draws a
parallel between the city of Vancouver and London, and by
implication, with the doomed city of Babylon. Long Will of
Langland may be, as Frye puts it, the voice of a "conservative-
radical opposition to oligarchy" who finds to his disgust a society
based on profiteering,[2] but his function as moral critic encompas-
ses a much broader field than that implied in Frye's description.
In addition to the seven deadly sins as they are expressed in the
modern city, Langland registers a number of crimes never even
conceived of in his own day. Unlike the episodes concerning
Vancouver's actual past, this section of the play attempts to examine Vancouver's success or failure in absolute rather than
comparative terms. It is not that the ills that Langland sees are
qualitatively different from those perceived by the Chief, Gassy
Jack, or Captain Vancouver; the difference is that Langland is

meticulously thorough in searching out the city's sins and is eloquently vehement in presenting them as evidence of the city's approaching damnation. Everywhere he turns, he finds pollution of the land and of minds; he sees the city's inhabitants living in isolation and unspectacular desperation:

> Yea there I saw a soft middle class swaddled in trees,
> In unfrequented churches, and in fears not a few,
> Chained as fast to profits as poorer folk to wages,
> Their roofs and hopes higher but higher still their mortgages.
> Some knew nobleness, and neighborly lived:
> Some had milk in morning to melt their bellies' ulcers,
> And rode alone to office, an ego to an auto.

He sees the "harried eyes" of the east end labourers, and the corruption that thrives and spreads among the city's casualties and failures, who also have their own territory:

> Softly in Powell Street, I heard the pimps whisper.
> And Cordova was lined with loggers and leggers,
> Honest men and reefers, rubadubs and bums—

Equally suspicious is he of the wealthy North Shore dwellers who are only predators of a higher order:

> Beyond the tamed shores that no tide cleansed
> Rose the raped mountains, scarred with fire and finance,
> And raddled with the lonely roofs of the rich,
> Of barristers and bookies and brokers aplenty,
> Of agents for septic tanks, for aspirin, or souls.
> Executives, crooners, con-men a few—

Significantly, there is ironic interplay between Langland and Legion. Langland takes the attitude that the evils of the city are an outgrowth of original sin and that only by the repudiation of present ways can an otherwise inevitable damnation be avoided. Legion, on the other hand, possesses precisely that quality of blind and unquestioning adherence to the city's false values which Langland condemns. Hence he can boast:

> Now—almost two million people!
> And our river, Mr. Long Will,
> May be dirty but it's busy,
> Every hundred yards a mill:

> Last year we got another
> Billion dollars out of trees.
> And there's salmon in that Fraser.
> Twenty million bucks from these.

His vulgar pride in wonders like the Plastickville Extension and his faith in his tourist propaganda as the gospel truth do more for Powers' cause and press Langland's argument far more than his own. It is true that Langland is frighteningly acute in his observation that

> . . . your folk that walk fat are fallen sick with fear,
> Taking but the time's toys and trashing all the future,
> Lunatic in laughter, lost in mere getting,
> And haunted by a skydoom their own hates have sealed.

Yet his vision must finally be found limited, puritanical, and debilitating; he sees the city's failures but not its hopes, its institutions, but not its dreams, its masses but not its individuals. As Mrs. Anyone remarks,

> His eyes were on the sins he loved to hate.
> He heard the bomb but not the children whistling.
> Yet children, grown, may sing a doom awry.
> He did not stay to see the selfless deeds that multiply
> And hum like simmering bees across my city's gardens,
> Storing for winter all that summer pardons.

Langland's sermon-like exhortation to Legion's world,

> . . . if ye lack love, all your living's lifeless,
> Love too of truth, and of your children yet to be,
> Love of joy and giving joy, and gaining love by loving,
> Lust for peace and man's mind and what men can do

is peculiarly ironic becuase Langland himself obviously is unable to practise what he preaches. His approach to the city of Vancouver, as to London, is relentlessly grim and unhopeful, and his attitude to humanity more scornful than loving.

The dialectic of Legion's argument for the preservation of the city and the witnesses' arguments for its damnation leads to the single seemingly firm conclusion that the city must be lost, that is, if it is to be judged by its failures. Vancouver is, for all of Legion's rationalizations and protest, a real conglomeration of icy commercialism, crime, grime, loneliness, phoniness, and many kinds of poverty. But none of the parties has looked at the city's inhabitants and individual human souls. That Birney delays the affirmation of the presence of a Life Force, embodied in Mrs. Anyone, until the end of the play seems a mite artificial in that the Life Force has been active throughout. But the play follows life in its recognition that it is the forces of destruction and negation that make the loudest and longest noises. The voice of Mrs. Anyone, emerging after the devastating evidence given in the preceding episodes of the play, is like the appearance of fireweed in a burned forest or bombed city. She is the green life which bursts through cracks in asphalt, and while admitting the evils and debilities of her world, she expresses what the dead, and therefore impartial and disinterested witnesses cannot know, namely the needs and hopes of people living now:

> For all mankind is matted so within me
> Despair can find no earth-room tall to grow;
> My veins run warm, however veers time's weather;
> I breathe Perhaps—May—but never—No.

Mrs. Anyone's vitality is bigger than that of Gassy Jack, Captain Vancouver, or the Salish Headman; she is not only receptive to nature and confident of her command of life, knowing that the future is what she makes each hour, she also possesses a larger understanding, rudimentary though it may be, of her own relationship with the time and space of the universe:

> Under the cool geyser of the dogwood
> Time lets me open books and live;
> Under the glittering comment of the planets
> Life asks, and I am made to give.

Mrs. Anyone represents the force of creative evolution, the soul of the free people for whom there is a continuing re-creation of wonder and meaning. Hence Powers' warning that

> Your world is armagadding;
> No conjury of little folk undoes its warlocks.
> You're now too billion many,

cannot defeat her creative willing, and she replies,

The more to want and thus to will—and then we've caught
it.
How many leaps of light away peace spins
The heart builds its long telescope to plot it.

She is also the Eve principle, and, as in *Paradise Lost* in
which Eve dreams of good while Michael tells Adam of coming
misery, Mrs. Anyone can also see good in the future even in the
shadow of evil:

Powers: (Moving to tower close over her.)
           But lady, lady, I threaten ever-the-lease.
Mrs. A.:   (With a head-toss.)
           How could I know, without the threat of death, I
           lived?
Powers: But do you know why you defy me?
Mrs. A.:   (Looking up almost tenderly at him.)
           That you might also be.
           Without my longer will, my stubborn boon,
           You'd have no mate to check with but the cor-
           nered moon.
           (Slowly) It's my defiant fear keeps green this
           whirling world.

Accepting the fact that we are condemned to live in the world
we have made, Mrs. Anyone treats life as a purgatorial quest for
the triumph of humanity through love and hope. That she dema-
terializes Legion is a metaphor for the endurance of her vitality as
it transcends and ultimately perhaps negates the more transient
mercantile values represented by Legion. The city is an organism,
and its protoplasm is not its institutions but the individuals in-
habiting it. Finally too, it is Powers, the principle now of just annihilation, of Death, who has only the skeleton and she who has
the key, and a life.

The city *per se* is buried in this final episode because Birney
does not try to offer a tailored solution to urban problems. The
affirmation of hope for mankind's continuing existence on earth
can be co-existent with symptoms of failure because, it is sug-
gested, it is not only by past mistakes that we are to be judged,
but also by our desires and our imaginations. History suspends
judgement but that is only to say that mankind is on continuing
trial. Birney's perception of what man has done to the earth is
acutely critical, even grim, but in the texture of the whole vision,

20

interwoven in the pattern of fear, guilt, and uncertainty is a strong humanism insisting on the possibility of growth and the autonomy of the human will. In the working notes for the play he writes:

> ... the faith I cling to, a stubborn but I hope not merely romantic faith in the enduring power of man himself to improve himself—man who, so long as he remains alive, may remake, any moment, his whole future; or even if that future must have an end in our sun's explosion or its dimming, has a present that can be glorious.

Wai Lan Low
LLB.II   Osgoode Hall Law School

---

[1]Northrop Frye, "Letters in Canada: Poetry, 1952-1960" in *Masks of Poetry: Canadian Critics on Canadian Verse*, ed. A. J. M. Smith (Toronto: McClelland & Stewart, 1962), p. 102.
[2]*Ibid.*, p. 103.

DAMNATION OF VANCOUVER

A Comedy in Seven Episodes

N.B. For suggestions as to costume, make-up, casting and character interpretation see Appendix

CHARACTERS

AT RISE OF CURTAIN

> *President* of the Hearing, and Minister of History
> *Clerk* of the Hearing
> Mr. P. S. *Legion*, Counsel for the Metropolis of Vancouver
> Mr. Gabriel *Powers*, Q.C., Counsel for the Office of the Future
> *Miss Take*, Stenographer

OTHERS, IN ORDER OF APPEARANCE

> Captain George *Vancouver*, Explorer, Pacific Northwest Coast, 1792
> *Skuh*-wath-kwuh-*tlath*-kyootl, *Chief* or Headman of the Snow-Kwee
>   Salish, 1792-1842
> Dr. E. O. *Seen*, a Professor of Geology at the University of the
>   Sovereign State of Columbia
> Mr. *Jack* C. Deighton (Gassy Jack), Proprietor of the Deighton
>   Arms, Gastown, 1882-86
> William *Langland*, author of "Piers Plowman", c. 1330-c. 1400
> *Mrs.* Anyone, a housewife

TIME

FIVE YEARS FROM NOW

SCENE

Platform of small hall in basement of Vancouver Court House. The five members of the Hearing are seated around a table littered with their equipment. *Miss Take* has a recorder, notebook, and compact; the *Clerk* a profusion of card files, papers, and a great iron key; *Legion* a heap of tourist pamphlets, law books, and a city directory; in front of *Powers* the bare table. Behind the table there is a large blackboard on stilts and a simulation of some automatic TV robot of five years from now. There is also a rostrum with shallow steps and a folding screen serving as a witness box. One exit leads to the ante-room. The other (right), black-draped and commanded by a spotlight, is the door of the ghosts.

EPISODE I

(At rise of curtain the members of the hearing are in their places around table, except for CLERK, *who is standing at automatic TV, poised, looking at his wrist watch.* PRESIDENT *(on rostrum) is doodling,* MISS TAKE *making up her face from compact,* LEGION *peering anxiously out at audience.* POWERS, *face practically hidden, gazes at the table.)*

CLERK: Ready, sir?

PRESIDENT: Eh? Eh? O yes.

CLERK: *(Rapidly punches buttons, turns handles, then looks at watch again.)* Auto-tele-mat set to telecast us in – fifteen seconds from – NOW. *(Punches one more button and scurries towards his seat.)*

PRESIDENT: Wait! Drat it, where in – *(Searches over his raised desk, looks wildly around.)* where's my gavel?

CLERK: *(Hurriedly deflects himself up rostrum steps, pulls gavel from under* PRESIDENT's *papers, hands it.)* Here sir! *(Leaps down and into seat.)*

PRESIDENT: Whew! Thanks! *(Pounds gavel and begins to speak in a somewhat bored, official voice.)* By the powers conferred on me as Minister of History in the Sovereign State of Columbia, I now convoke, on this tenth day of February, nineteen hundred and whatever-it-is-plus-five, in the Metropolis of Vancouver, a Public Hearing to consider any objections to the proposal to eliminate the said metropolis. Notice of objection having been duly filed by the Metropolis of Vancouver itself, my government has consented to the appearance here today of Counsel for the Metropolis – *(Waves gavel somewhat resignedly at* LEGION.) Mr. P. S. Legion. Humm. These proceedings are, as you see *(Looks at* MISS TAKE.) being properly taken down, taped, *(Looks along table.)* broadcast and *(Waving gavel at autotelemat.)* telecast. *(Bangs gavel and proceeds more briskly.)* And now let's get on with it. Mr. Legion, if you've anything to say on behalf of Vancouver, this is the time.

LEGION: (*Rises, turns toward* PRESIDENT *with air of shocked disapproval.*)
Really, Mr. President,
   This seems to me irregular.
I don't know what you're pulling,
   But I hope it's not our leg you are.

PRESIDENT: (*Blandly.*) Come now, Mr. Legion, I know this isn't exactly a Court of Law, but it *is* a Public Hearing, and you might preserve a little private dignity.

LEGION: What's the use of dignity? How can we discuss?! (*Gestures at audience – the supposedly, but let us hope not actually, empty hall.*) Why, there isn't any public here but us! (*Sits disgustedly.*)

PRESIDENT: Dear, dear, you lack confidence in your clients, Mr. Legion. This hall may be empty but don't forget (*Gestures at autotelemat.*) our friend Auto. You wouldn't expect a Vancouverite to come all the way down in the rain to this Court House cellar when any chair at home is softer? At any rate, I'm here, and you're here and (*Gestures.*) the Clerk of the Hearing (*He is scrabbling at files.*) and the stenographer (*She simpers.*) and – (*Pauses, looks down at* POWERS, *who continues to gaze unmoved at the table.*) Counsel for the State. (*Looks smilingly at* LEGION *and then at autotelemat.*) Everything is beautifully regular.

LEGION: (*Springs up again.*)
Regular?! When someone is proposing, sir –
   And no one *has* said who –
To eliminate my clients?
   Who wants to? Is it you? (*Sits.*)

PRESIDENT: I? Of course not. (*Makes a Pontius Pilate gesture of washing his hands.*) I'm neutral. The proposal I may say, comes from a, umm, a *new* department in our government, the –

LEGION: (*Jumps up, interrupting, gesturing demagogically to his unseen audience behind the autotelemat.*) A new one! Another! This is all mighty queer –

PRESIDENT: (*Continuing blandly.*) The office of the Future.

LEGION: (*A little taken aback.*) The Future! Who – Who runs it? (*Recovering his aggressiveness.*) And why aren't they here? (*Sits.*)

PRESIDENT: Naturally there's no one present from the Future. But (*Suave gesture with gavel.*) Our learned Queen's Counsel, Mr. Gabriel Powers, is here, of Queendom, Powers, Prince, and Policy. You hold a brief for the Office of the Future, I believe, Mr. Powers?

POWERS: (*At last he joins the party, rises, bows to* PRESIDENT.) Yes sir, I hold a watching, waiting, all-too-brief.

LEGION: (*Up.*) What? What's that, Mr. – Mr. Powers? *You're* waiting? It's we who wait
To learn what grisly, unnatural fate
You propose for this city – and when, sir – and why?

POWERS: Somewhen the Future will, and no why sooner,
Damn, most god-naturely, Vancouver. (*Sits calmly.*)

LEGION: (*Confused, to* POWERS.) What's that? I didn't catch –

CLERK: (*Turning to* MISS TAKE.) Did he say 'damn'?

MISS TAKE: (*Plaintively.*) (*To* PRESIDENT) Please, sir –

LEGION: (*Looking wildly around.*) Good — god-naturely – dam – ?

MISS TAKE: Please, how –

PRESIDENT: (*Bangs gavel.*) Language, Mr. Legion! Ladies present.

LEGION: I didn't say it first, I just wanted to know which dam –

MISS TAKE: Please, sir (*Waving her book at* PRESIDENT.) –

PRESIDENT: (*With martyred patience.*) Yes, Miss Take.

MISS TAKE: How am I to spell that – that word?

LEGION: (*With indignant innocence, flouncing back to his seat.*) That's all *I* wanted to know.

PRESIDENT: A fair question . . . Mr. Powers?

POWERS: (*Showing, for the first time, his steely intention.*) With a D, A, M, *and* an N – or spell it dim – or doom – it is damnation we purpoise.

LEGION: (*Staring across bewildered at* POWERS.) Pur – - Pur-*poise* you said? (*Bangs one of own ears.*)

POWERS: (*Helps out with a sinister gesture of poising.*) Purpoise.

MISS TAKE: Please sir, how do I spell – ?

PRESIDENT: (*Quickly.*) Don't try. It's all going down on your tape recorder. Work it out from that tomorrow.

MISS TAKE: (*Unconvinced but humouring him.*) Yes, sir.

LEGION: (*Surveying them all.*) Look, what's going on? What's all this doubletalk? (*Disgustedly.*) "Purpoise!"

POWERS: (*Patiently, as to a child.*)We poise our purpose, since our Judgement Deed is still undayed.

LEGION: (*Banging table.*) *Mister* Powers, let's talk plain English. I want a straight answer to –

PRESIDENT: I'm afraid, Mr. Legion, you'll have to cash Mr. Powers' words at par. He has been briefed by the Office of the *Future*, remember? Well, then he must use the Future's language. It's not *his* fault if English has gone and changed again.

LEGION: (*Flustered, he bangs table again.*)
I don't care what he talks, he must give us a reason.
Dim, dam, this country's greatest city? Why
that's – that's treason!

POWERS: (*Rises.*) Treason or true, the Off-face of the Future
finds this city-pretty now a misfate in its planes.
Like every think of booty, sir,
it's copulated to destriction;
its lifeliness decreases and must ever
pass into nothingmist.
Your town's dimnition is, I fear,
inevitoidable, and overdue. (*Sits.*)

LEGION: My learned friend speaks gibberish
　　　　To hide a government plot,
　　　But my two million clients will insist
　　　　He tells us all what's what.
　　　It's rumoured a Cabinet motion was passed
　　　To experiment here with a Zee-Bomb Blast.
　　　But the Cabinet's gone fishing, all the Senate too,
　　　And here you sit and talk of dams – what *are* you
　　　　　　　　trying to do?

POWERS: The Vee-dails of the doomning, Mr. Bleegion,
　　　Are not yet warred out foully,
　　　Nor would it be within the public in-rest
　　　To diverge them now.

LEGION: (*Jumps up with calculated theatrics, pounds fist, glowers at*
　　　PRESIDENT.)
　　　This Hearing's all a farce!
　　　(*Goes and pounds table near Powers.*)
　　　You can't speak English well enough
　　　To tell us where or why
　　　Or how or when you want to-to-to damn –
　　　So you've got no right to try!
　　　(*Walks back disgusted and sits.*)

PRESIDENT: (*Wearily.*) O come now, Mr. Legion, we're here to consider
　　　objections to the plan, not to the planners. The Future has the
　　　right to damn.

LEGION: (*Up on his feet, mad this time.*)
　　　The right! Who gave it to them?

PRESIDENT: (*As if trying to recall.*) Umm, let's see – o yes, (*Brightly.*) it was
　　　the Minister of History.

LEGION: (*Fit to be tied.*) The Minister of History! That's you!

PRESIDENT: That's true.

LEGION: (*Marches back to his place, picks up papers.*)
　　　I demand another venue.

PRESIDENT: (*Cheerfully firm.*) There is no other, this must do.
　　　Please order from the menu.

LEGION: (*Bangs papers down.*)
My clients do not think, sir, this is a laughing matter.

PRESIDENT: No more it is, – for them. (*Briskly.*) So let's cut out the chatter.

LEGION: Now who's undignified? My clients, sir, object –

PRESIDENT: My dear Mr. Legion, we know they object. But have you any *unbiased* person ready to support their objections?

LEGION: (*Confident again, grabs up sheet of paper by his chair.*)
I've thirty waiting in the ante-room (*Gestures left.*)
And every one a leading citizen:
Two brigadiers, a broker and five lumbermen,
The Mayor, the Lions' newest coach, and –

PRESIDENT: Sorry, not allowed.

LEGION: What!

PRESIDENT: Obviously biased persons, they're all – technically at least – alive.

LEGION: A-alive? (*Decides to laugh it off as a joke.*) Yeh, yeh, sure. (*Double take.*) What?

PRESIDENT: My ministry has ruled that only the dead are neutral. Have you no dead on that list?

LEGION: (*Automatically looks at his list then flings it on table. In a rage.*)
Dead! Of course I haven't any dead! O this is (*Spluttering.*) ridiculous! Insane! Illegal! I-I (*Shouting.*) won't go on. You –

MISS TAKE: (*Having trouble with the levels of her tape recorder.*) Oh, oh, please, Mr. Legion –

PRESIDENT: Temper, temper, Mr. Legion. Everything will be all right. You see, as Minister of History, I'm empowered to raise the dead – that is, for the purposes of giving testimony.

MISS TAKE: (*Squeaks.*) The dead!

LEGION: (*Slumping into his chair disgustedly.*) The Dead.

CLERK: (*Shifting to another card index imperturbably.*)
Yessir, materialization file ready.

PRESIDENT: We'll have them fade away as soon as we've finished with them (*Looking around the table reassuringly.*) and we won't allow more than one of them to hang around at a time. (*Briskly.*) Now, Mr. Legion, who would you like to start with?

LEGION: (*Slowly.*) Who ... would I ... ? Look, I don't *know* any dead. I-I'm not prepared, I-I'll need a recess to –

PRESIDENT: Recesses not allowed.

LEGION: (*Groans.*)

PRESIDENT: Besides, your chances are as good as Mr. Powers'. . . .
And you're not objecting, are you, Mr. Powers?

POWERS: Not in the sly-list, Mr. Prosy-dent.

LEGION: Yeah. He's got an "in" on the Future.

PRESIDENT: Ah, but even the Future's lawyer can't be certain what the Past thinks.

LEGION: (*Groans.*)

PRESIDENT: If you'd like a suggestion, Mr. Legion – why not start with your clients' namesake?

LEGION: Who?

PRESIDENT: Vancouver. Captain George Vancouver. Your grand-foster-parent. His views might prove interesting.

LEGION: Saay, they might at that. (*Quickly suspicious.*)
Wait, you've been talking to him.

PRESIDENT: Cross my heart, no. This would be absolutely his first appearance on any panel.

LEGION: Well . . . all right. But I reserve notice of appeal.

PRESIDENT: No appeals. And now (*Casually, as if he were asking for the window to be shut.*) will the Clerk please ask Captain Vancouver to materialize . . . ?

CLERK: (*Bustles off to* RIGHT *exit.*) Captain Vancouver! . . . Captain Vancouver!

VANCOUVER: (*OFF RIGHT, after pause.*) Aye, aye, sirs!

CLERK: Please materialize this way.

VANCOUVER: (*Nearer OFF*) Coming!

STAGE BLACKS OUT

EPISODE 2

(VANCOUVER *appears suddenly in spot RIGHT. LIGHTS UP.* CLERK *at once trots back to seat,* MISS TAKE *gives a little squeal, and* LEGION *rises in excitement.* VANCOUVER *walks in FRONT of* POWERS *to FRONT CENTRE and bows to* PRESIDENT, *sweeping off his hat.*)

VANCOUVER: Your sarvant, sir.

PRESIDENT: Welcome back, Captain. Mr. Legion here would like to ask you some questions.

VANCOUVER: (*Bows to* LEGION *who is now striding around table towards him.*) Sarvant, sir. Fire ahead.

LEGION: (*Seizes* VANCOUVER's *hand.*) You – you really *are* Captain Vancouver, Captain George Vancouver? (*Pumping hand.*) I'm honoured, honoured to meet you, Captain. And my congratulations.

MISS TAKE: (*Is smitten with the Captain as he passes her.*) Gosh!

VANCOUVER: Congratulations?

LEGION: (*Dropping* VANCOUVER's *hand he puts his arm chummily over* VANCOUVER's *shoulder and steers him around table LEFT to witness box, talking rapidly and enthusiastically.*) Why certainly, sir, you started it all. You discovered Burrard Inlet, Bowen Island, Mt. Baker – the works. Now there's millions of us Vancouverites – *your* descendants –

VANCOUVER: (*Freeing himself gently.*) Oh, I say, not really all my descendants.

LEGION: Sure, this is Vancouver, Captain. I'm a Vancouverite, so is the Clerk here (*Gestures at* CLERK *who, instead of taking a bow, merely nods and goes back to studying his files.*) and so is our lovely Miss Take (*She preens and beams.*) – and so are you, Captain –

VANCOUVER: No!

32

LEGION: Our first citizen – well (*Seeing him about to demur.*) our first white citizen, eh, Captain?

VANCOUVER: (*Takes his stand in witness box.* LEGION *stands close to him.*)
I happened to explore this inlet, true;
I think that was in seventeen ninety-two?

LEGION: It was, Captain, it was (*Switching to the solemn.*) And now sir, aren't you horror struck to learn that there are people threatening to put an end to this beautiful city you began?

POWERS: A loaded question, Mr. Leading – but no matter.

VANCOUVER: Did I begin it? Faith it was by chance.
My orders were to chart the northwest main
And find if any strait led home again.
I had to navigate the lot to say
If none gave passage back to Hudson's Bay.
Bemused with this, I never, more's the pity,
Foresaw along these shaggy cliffs a city.

LEGION: (*Laughing that one off with a pat to* VANCOUVER's *back.*)
I see you're modest, Captain, but I'm sure
You're pleased to see the names of many a friend,
Living forever round our city's shores –
Unless (*Scowl at* POWERS.) this government contrives its end.
I hope you've looked around our U.S.S.C.,
Columbia's fastest growing university,
Complete with totem poles, tetanus farms,
Canned TV lectures, rocket alarms –
Bigger than Oxford, and the co-eds – saaay –

VANCOUVER: (*Gallant nod to* MISS TAKE.) Doubtless as fetching as the belles of my day.

LEGION: Ten thousand science grads a year!

VANCOUVER: But less than twenty humanists, I hear.

LEGION: (*Doesn't understand the word.*) Hume – ? Uh, sure,
But what about our port, that every seadog praises?
You wouldn't want to see *it* blown to blazes?

VANCOUVER: I'll wager Burrard's proud to know his harbour
Is toothed with docks from lar- to star-board;
But all this town – these gross mechanic jaws
That clamp and champ around the sea – what was
Your question, sir, again? –

POWERS: You can load a Captain to the water, but you can't make him sink.

LEGION: What? What's that? (*Decides to ignore* POWERS.)
My dear Captain, let the question be:
If you would like to see
This great metropolis,
The West's unique Acropolis,
Blown up? Blown down? H-bombed?! Zee-bopped?!

POWERS: (*Rising*) Your question's once again misleading, Mr. Logion.
Our method of bomb-nation's not yet subtled. However, Captain (*Sitting again, gesturing at* VANCOUVER.), pray Pray-cede.

VANCOUVER: (*Musing, trying to be fair.*)
Hmm, I'm not the sort who likes to see things go –
But what I saw, sirs, went some time ago;
Those paddling Indians who held a forum
Around our ship – with what a proud decorum
They shared their feast with us – some smelts they'd cooked;
Their Chief sat like Apollo bronzed, yet looked,
Poor soul, on me as if I were the god –
It seems his race is mostly under sod?

LEGION: (*Trying to be hearty and reassuring.*)
Lord no, we've hundreds yet. They're gutting
Fish for our tremendous canning trade –
Or living off the State. They're Christians, too,
They even vote. Don't fret, they've made the grade.

POWERS: (*Rising, with scorn.*) Objaculation, Mr. Minister! My wordy friend sleeks to misleed the Captain into thinking-thanking bleak is white, and grade disgrade, and every needive snug in his Prochristean bed.

PRESIDENT: No doubt, no doubt, but Captain Vancouver seems able to form his own judgements, Mr. Powers. (POWERS *sits*.) However, we might, when the Captain's finished, call up that decorous Apollo himself, the Redskin chief he was talking about, and get his side of it.

34

LEGION: Side? I object. He hasn't a side, he's a side issue.

PRESIDENT: Tut-tut, Mr. Legion . . . Mr. Powers?

POWERS: No objection. An excellent propuzzle, sir, most aboriginal.

PRESIDENT: Right! Objection over-ruled, Mr. Legion. And now get on with your own witness.

LEGION: (*Sighs.*) Look, Captain, it's us whites that really matter;
We built this mighty city in your name;
Three generations hacked it from the timber –
You wouldn't want to see it end in flame?

VANCOUVER: (*Bored with role* LEGION *is trying to make him play, decides to wind it up.*)
A feat indeed in such a trifling time
To piece together so much wood – and grime;
'Tis huge as my old Lunnon, and as dun,
As planless, not so plaguey – but less fun.
I rather liked the sweep of fir and cedar.
Your city? Sir, I can't think why we need her.

LEGION: (*Betrayed, goes and sits, casting disgusted glance at* PRESIDENT.)
Grand-foster-parent! (*Surly nod to* POWERS.) Your witness, Mr. Powers.

POWERS: Thank you, Mr. Leed-won, but you've pre-formed all criss-cross-examinations necessary. Nor need the Future ask a reckoning of this Captaive. He chased, he beached the white whale, yet never stayed to watch him puff with death-in-life nor ever cares the time has come to bury Moby, not appraise him. (*Sits*)

PRESIDENT: (*Brisk again.*) Very well then, will the Clerk please dematerialize Captain Vancouver. Thank you, Captain. (VANCOUVER *bows.* CLERK *conducts him* LEFT *around* LEGION *then* RIGHT *across front of stage to* RIGHT *exit.* MISS TAKE *looks sad as he passes her.*)

CLERK: This way. (VANCOUVER *stands by* RIGHT *exit.* LIGHTS OUT. *Spot on* VANCOUVER.) Captain Vancouver, please dematerialize.

VANCOUVER: (*Final bow.*) Your sarvant, all. (*Spot out.* VANCOUVER *exits in dark. Then calls, OFF.*) God send safe harbourage.

EPISODE 3

LIGHTS UP

(CLERK *trots calmly back to seat.* LEGION *is sunk in disgusted apathy.*)

PRESIDENT: (*Rubbing hands.*) Well now, who's next? Mr. Legion, it's time *you* picked somebody from history's pocket. What about an early mayor? A Caribou Trailer? No? A missionary? Hmm. Ah, I have it, we forgot the Indian chief. The Clerk will look up his file.

LEGION: (*Jumping up.*)
Mr. Minister, I must protest procedure so unfair.
I've had no time to see these – these ghouls
beforehand, and prepare.
I –

PRESIDENT: O now you want everything dull and logical, Mr. Legion. Always remember that Mr. Powers is under the same disadvantages I impose on you.

LEGION: Well let *him* call a witness, while I think. (*Sits.*)

POWERS: By all moons let us help my wearthy Coll-ide think, and moantime softly salmon up the Chief.

LEGION: Wait! I reserve the right to cross-examine.

PRESIDENT: Agreed, Mr. Powers?

POWERS: I'm happy all-wise to leave the inter-corruptions to opposing Counsel.

PRESIDENT: Err, fine: Now Mr. Clerk, you've found the right Chief?

CLERK: (*Peering at a card he has been searching for.*) Seventeen-ninety-two, Burrard Inlet. Tribe contacted by Captain Vancouver was Snow-kwee Salish. Headman was Skwath – (*Chokes on it.*) Skwath something, sir.

36

PRESIDENT: Have him materialize.

    CLERK: (*Trots deadpan over behind* PRESIDENT *to exit RIGHT and calls.*)
Headman, Snow-skwee, So-kwee, no Snow-kwee Salish, seven-
teen ninety-two. Headman Skwath; please materialize this way.
LIGHTS DOWN

    CHIEF: (*Appears suddenly in spot. LIGHTS UP.* CHIEF *silently follows*
CLERK *to front CENTRE, and faces* PRESIDENT. MISS TAKE *gasps
and looks bug-eyed, contriving to maintain this attitude to* CHIEF
throughout.) Peace to my cousins.

PRESIDENT: Welcome, Chief.

    CLERK: This way. (*Leads* CHIEF *around LEFT past* LEGION, *who glowers
mistrustfully at him, to witness box.* CLERK *resumes seat, takes
up pen.*) Name please.

    CHIEF: *Skuh*-wath-kwuh-*tlath*-kyootl.

MISS TAKE: Please, Mr. President –

    CLERK: Skuh – uh?

MISS TAKE: How am I to spell *that*?!

    CHIEF: Call me Chief.

    CLERK: (*To* MISS TAKE, *as he writes.*) Chief. C-H-E-I-F.

MISS TAKE: (*Writing.*) Gee, thanks.

PRESIDENT: Chief, I understand you were Headman when Captain Vancouver sailed into Burrard Inlet.

    CHIEF: And fifty summers more, after he sailed away.
It was in the green shooting of my chieftainship
His cloudboat came.

PRESIDENT: Good. We're presuming, Chief, you've kept abreast of happen-
ings around the Inlet since your own, umm, departure.

CHIEF: I have watched, sir, the snow of my people melt
Under the white man's summer.

PRESIDENT: Aye, no doubt. And you understand the issues being debated
at this Hearing?

CHIEF: Where once we hunted, white men have built many longhouses,
But they move uneasy as mice within them.
They have made slaves from waterfalls
And magic from the souls of rocks.
They are stronger than grizzlies.
But their slaves bully them,
And they are chickadees in council.
Some of you say (*Turning towards* LEGION.): "Give us time,
We will grow wise, and invent peace."
(*Turning to* POWERS.)
Others say: "The sun slides into the saltchuk;
We must follow the Redman into the trail of darkness."

PRESIDENT: Any objections to this summation, gentlemen?

POWERS: Abject to such objectiveness? Hidman, toll your story.

LEGION: (*Rising.*) Well *I* object! How can he understand?
He's just a – a primitive, a redskin, a pagan stone-age man!

PRESIDENT: Chief, do you feel capable of advising us?

CHIEF: Yea, are we not all sons of the same brown Asia tribe?
My fathers, roaming ever eastward,
Crossed Bering, made human half the world.
Your fathers, whitening over Europe,
And ever westering, circled back to us,
Bringing us your woes, clasped in your totems,
Carved in those Powers of lead and steel
We had not known, unknowing had not lacked,
Yet from the knowing needed.

LEGION: (*Moving close to* CHIEF, *with chummy condescension.*)
O come you always needed us; we had the know-how.
Before the whites, the Siwash was a lowbrow.

38

CHIEF: Before the tall ships tossed their shining tools to us
My uncle was our carpenter.
With saw of flame he laid the great cedars low,
Split the sweet-smelling planks with adze of jade,
Bowed them his way with steam and thong,
Shaped the long wind-silvered house
Where fifty of my kin and I lived warm as bear.
He hollowed the great canoes we rode the gulf in, safe as gulls.
My uncle had a Guarding Power with Brother Wood.

LEGION: You got along somehow (*Going back towards seat.*), that's
all you really mean.
(*Turning on him.*) But honest now, you had it tough until we
hit the scene.
For instance, is it true or not –
You fellows couldn't even make a pot?

CHIEF: Red roots and yellow weeds entwined themselves
Within our women's hands, coiled to those baskets darting
With the grey wave's pattern, or the wings
Of dragonflies, you keep in your great cities now
Within glass boxes. Now they are art, white man's taboo,
But once they held sweet water.

LEGION: Give me an aluminum pressure cooker anytime. (*Sits.*)

CHIEF: It is swift indeed, as lava springs,
But it does not have our wave pattern.

LEGION: That's all very well, the things you'd eat.
You never learned to farm, just wolfed raw fish and meat.
One day a feast and the next day a famine.
Why you'd all have starved if there hadn't been salmon.

CHIEF: Salmon was bread.
When in the Tide of Thimbleberries
The first silverback threshed in our dipnets
                    My father's drum called all the village.
(*Drum beat begins softly off stage and gradually increases in
tempo and intensity.*)
The red flesh flaked steaming from the ceremonial spit.
My father chanted thanks to the Salmon Power,
and everyone in turn tasted bird-like.

We young men ran to the water.
The bows of our canoes returning were flecked like mica.
With flying fingers the women split the shiny ones,
Hung them on cunning cedar racks,
So that our friends, the air and the sun,
Might seal the good oils for the winter storing.
Salmon was bread.

(*Drum stops.*)

LEGION: (*Sniffs.*) Fish!

CHIEF: (*Ignoring him.*)
But there were nights we returned from the mountains
With deer on our shoulders,
Or from the still coves with ducks.
Then all the longhouses made music,
There was roasting of spicy roots,
There were sweet small plums,
The green shoots of vines, and lily bulbs
That grew for us unprompted.
– It was not till *your* time, sir (*Turning to* LEGION),
I saw a Salish go hungry.

POWERS: (*To* LEGION.) You have been faithfully unsirred, my
leer-ed friend.

LEGION: (*Jumps up.*) Yahhh, you're falling for a corny Hiawatha line.
I'm through with this witness; he's wasting our time.
(*Sits.*)

POWERS: (*Rising slowly.*) All time's a waste of Hiawathas; let this brown
whiteness, Mr. Mine-ister, tell on *his* time and waste.

PRESIDENT: (*Shrugs.*) If you wish; but he might perhaps keep closer to the
point.

POWERS: (*Forcefully.*) Our wheatman's present is impaled upon his village point. He loved as long, lived better. (*Sits.*)

LEGION: My learned friend sets highest store
By what goes down our throats.
I'm defending civilization –
Not a camp of fishing boats.

40

CHIEF: (*Sunk in his memories, not speaking to any of them especially.*)
There was more, a something – I do not know –
A way of life that died for yours to live.
We gambled with sticks, and storms, and wives, but we
did not steal.
The Chief my father spoke to the people only what was true.
When there was quarrel, he made us unravel it with reason,
Or wrestle weaponless on the clean sand.
We kept no longhouses for warriors, we set no state over
others.
Each had his work, and all made certain each was fed.
It was a way –

LEGION: (*Up.*) But it wasn't any way to build *security*!
You fellows never got things straight,
You never thought in terms of *government*,
You ought at least have tried a tribal super-state.
Now we've a *culture*, built on (*He's not too sure what.*) –
on, well
Thousands of years of – of thinking.

CHIEF: (*He has begun to wander LEFT past LEGION and around table's
end to FRONT, musing. LEGION keeps an uneasy eye on him.*)
Sometimes a young man would be many months thinking,
Alone in the woods as a heron,
And learning the Powers of the creatures.
When I was young I lay and watched the little grey doctor,
The lizard, I studied his spirit, I found his song,
When I was Chief (*With a touch of pride.*) I carved him on
my house-posts.
I took the red earths and the white, and painted his wisdom.

LEGION: (*Waving at him.*) Gentlemen, you see! Superstition, totem,
tá-boo.
This testimony's worthless, a bunch of old voodoo.

CHIEF: (*Looking sardonically at LEGION.*)
It is true we saw threats and marvels in all that moved,
But we had no god whose blood must be drunk,
Nor a hell for our enemies.
These the white man brought us.

41

LEGION: Objection, Mr. Minister.
       This is a Christian court.
He's got no right to make such cracks,
       It's time you cut him short.

PRESIDENT: Umm, well, this is a Hearing not a Court, Mr. Legion, a more-
or-less Christian Hearing, I suppose, but the witnesses aren't
sworn. However, if you've no more questions, I –

LEGION: Wait, yes I have. (*Slyly.*)
Chief, will you tell us, pray,
       If all you Siwash –

CHIEF: Salish, please.

LEGION: *All* right, Salish –
       If all you Salish were so smart,
How come you threw your goods away?
       Potlatches? Remember? Give your shirt off your back
And beg for it back the very next day? (*Sits.*)

CHIEF: (*Pacing slowly across FRONT, rapt in recall.*)
Like dolphin our kindred came, arching over the waves.
My father stood tall on the house-roof,
Threw down soft cloaks of marten and mink,
White rugs of the wild goat's wool,
Tossed down, for the catching, red capes of the cedar bark,
And root-mats brown as the last cloud
In the sun's down-going.
The men made jokes, there was squirrel-chatter of women.
(*Pause*)
After, at the full tide's brim, they danced,
And my father put on the great-eyed mask of his Power,
With his secret kelp whistle spoke owl-words as he swayed.

(*Drum again off stage, following the rhythms and rising and
fallings of the* CHIEF's *words.*)

My uncle held his drum close to a tide-pool,
Rubbed the skin cunningly with his hands,
Made the downy whoosh of the owl in the night.
A shaman drew frog-talk from cockleshells
Hidden in the pool of his fingers.

42

The old men sang of the great chiefs that had been,
Their songs dying as wind, then swelling
As the carved rattles clacked,
As the shell-hoops spoke to the ritual sticks. . . .
Once there was silence . . . no one stirred. . . .
I heard the beat of my heart. . . .
Then like an arrow's thud one beat of the drum, one . . .
And one (*Growing faster*) . . . and one . . . and one
And suddenly all the drums were thunder
And everyone leaped singing and surging in the last dance. . . .

(*Drum suddenly stops.*)
(*Pause.*)

That was my first potlatch.

(*General silence, all gazing, moved, at* CHIEF. *He comes out of reverie and walks back to witness box.* LEGION *is first to recover, rises.*)

LEGION: Well . . . that was quite a party. . . . But then came the dawn
And your old man with a hangover, and not a shirt to pawn.

CHIEF: (*Turns bitterly on* LEGION.)
In those days we drank only our sounds.
We gave, and we were given to.
But when your fathers took our food and left us
                    little coins,
And when your shamans took our songs and left us
                    little hymns,
The music and the Potlatch stopped.

LEGION: I give up. You're full of moonshine and romance;
You never learned the meaning of that great word "advance."
Yet you lived till 1850 – did you never realize
What it meant to build this nation, to grow up,
                    to civilize?

CHIEF: When the strangers came to build in our village
I had two sons.
One died black and gasping with smallpox.
To the other the trader sold a flintlock.
My son gave the gun's height in otter skins.
He could shoot deer now my arrows fainted to reach.
One day he walked into the new whiskey-house
Your fathers built for us.
He drank its madness, he had the gun,
He killed his cousin, my brother's firstborn . . .
The strangers choked my son with a rope.
    From that day there was no growing in my nation.

LEGION: (*Clucks with routine sympathy.*) Too bad, too bad.
But a Chief like you, you had other kids?

CHIEF: I had a daughter. She died young, and barren
From the secret rot of a sailor's thighs.

LEGION: Hmm. (*At last he has no reply, sits.*)

PRESIDENT: (*Quietly.*) No more questions, Mr. Legion?
(LEGION *shakes his head.*) Mr. Powers?

POWERS: (*Rises.*) One only. . . . Old Chief and Challenge, toll
us your own end.

CHIEF: When the measles passed from our village
There were ninety to lift into the burial grove.
But the loggers had felled our trees,
There was only the cold earth, and nine men left to dig.
The doctor set fire to the longhouses and the carvings.
My cousins paddled me over the Sound
To sit alone by their smokehouse fire, for I, their Chief,
    was blind.
One night I felt with shuffling feet the beach-trail.
I walked into the saltwater,
I walked down to the home of the Seal Brother. . . .

PRESIDENT: (*After general silence.*) Thank you, Chief. There are no more
questions?

POWERS: None. Your doom's long paid, O hewed man. (*Looking at* LEGION.) The questions now are put to those who chiefly cancered yours.

(PRESIDENT *nods to* CLERK, *who rises. All rise.*)

CLERK: (*Beckoning and leading* CHIEF *to RIGHT EXIT, intoning.*) Please de-materialize this way, Chief.

(*LIGHTS DIM. CHIEF IN SPOT.*)

CHIEF: Peace to my cousins, comfort (*SPOT OUT*) and peace.

(*LIGHTS UP*)
(*All resume seats in silence except* POWERS, *who surveys the table from near his seat.*)

POWERS: From the ash of the fir springs the fire-weed;
From the ask of his faring your fear.
His village did not die that Legion's might
More losty lift, but that you might be meek
To understay your own swift Inding. (*Sits.*)

LEGION: (*Up and recovered.*)
You think because we built Vancouver on his campsite
We're going to let you knock it down? (*Laughs.*)
Give up our global future for a damsite?
Come off! We've just begun to build this town!

POWERS: What would you do with time but teem?

LEGION: Do? You wait and see! Someday we'll be
The universe's capital, the solar super-city.
It took two billion years to get things ready for us –
We want another billion in the kitty.

POWERS: The Office of the Future, Mr. Breegion, is not prepowered to ante more than five.

LEGION: Five? Five years? (POWERS *nods.* LEGION *turns to the* PRESIDENT.)
Mr. Minister, I've got an expert witness still outside,
A geologist (*Seeing* PRESIDENT *shaking his head.*) –
O.K., he's *technically* alive,
But I had him stay in case this point came up.
I must produce him – *please* – to show we need more years
than five.

PRESIDENT: A geologist?

LEGION: Perfessor Seen, sir, from U.S.S.C. A scientist. Impartial!
He lives *out*side the city in the lowest rental housing –
No vote, investment, bank account – no boosting and
no grousing.

PRESIDENT: Hmmm, I think, Mr. Powers, we might count him as one of the
dead, for our purposes? Any objections if we let the rule slide
this once?

POWERS: Sliderule or transit, all geologic works for me.
Agreed.

PRESIDENT: (*To* CLERK.) You may call Professor Seen from the anteroom.

CLERK: (*Scurries to LEFT EXIT and calls.*)
Prof. Seen. . . . Prof. Seen. (LEGION *sits.*)

EPISODE 4

SEEN: (*Off stage.*) Yes, yes . . . Coming . . . (*Enters and follows* CLERK *to witness box. He clutches a sheaf of notes in his hand.*)

CLERK: This way, Prof.

PRESIDENT: Good afternoon, Professor, sorry to have kept you waiting.

SEEN: (*Amiably.*) Not at all, not at all. (*Stands in box, looks at* LEGION *who is all smiles.*) It was nice of you to –

CLERK: (*Sits and meticulously interrupts.*) Full name, please.

(MISS TAKE *decides* SEEN *is not her type and goes to work on her nails.*)

SEEN: O, yes, sorry, Seen, S-E-E-N, Edward Oscar, Doctor E.O. Seen.

PRESIDENT: Your witness, Mr. Legion.

LEGION: (*Up and rubbing his hands.*)
Now, perfessor! Would you tell us first the story
    Of how Vancouver's setting was created,
How long it took to shape this trillion-dollar site
    That powerful Interests want annihilated.

POWERS: (*Interjecting sardonically.*) Or interested Powers.

SEEN: (*Off on a well-rehearsed speech, with occasional recourse to his notes.*)
From planet's birth, two billion years perhaps
    Till these shores shook, roared shuddering,
Hurled lava fuming four miles high,
    Built batholiths from Wenatchee to Yukon.

MISS TAKE: (*Has started note-taking belatedly and is having trouble.*) Bath-?
(*But no one notices her signals and she throws down her pencil and, bored, goes back to her nails.*)

SEEN: Then sixty million more for –

LEGION: Wait! (*Hops over to blackboard and chalks up in big letters:*
"2,000,000,000 years" *and under that "60,000,000". He continues
to keep tally.*)

SEEN: Sixty million more for mountains to chill,
Grow soil-skin, suffer valleys,
Till warping from palms went the winged lizards.

LEGION: Two billion, sixty million. (*Gleefully.*) Next?

SEEN: Twenty million years for such monsters to pass
While southward volcanoes seethed to the sky-vault,
Rainier and Baker rained rivers of breccia,
And sly cats grew into sabre-toothed tigers.

LEGION: (*Chalking up, and adding happily in his head.*)
Two billion, eighty million. Next, please!

SEEN: (*Glance at notes.*) And then a mere million of summers
As slowly clouds thicken, airs cool, falls the snow.
Magnolias moulder now under the ice-mounds
While south move the hairy ones, mammoth and mastodon.

LEGION: (*Adds a million.*) And Vancouver? What's it like here?

SEEN: Here incubus ice arcs over all,
Licks out fjords, levels the lean peaks.
Melts then, letting land rise.
Yet thrice inches forward, thrice wastes away.
Since last the glaciers shrank to the Pole
Count twenty milleniums, thirty it may be,
For first firs to flourish, and deer to find them,
For berries and bears, partridge in bracken.

LEGION: (*Adding "30,000" and a temporary total.*)
Two billion, eighty-one million, and thirty thousand years.
Gentlemen, you see! *And not even Man yet!* Tell us Perfessor,
how long since man?

SEEN: Since brown longheads leaped across Bering,
Slid down these coasts spearing the salmon,
At the most, two hundred centuries have hovered.

(LEGION *adds "20,000" under his previous total, then, with a flourish, the final total, while* SEEN *speaks another line.*)

SEEN: Man, sirs, this morning moved down to visit.

LEGION: (*Swings over and grasps* SEEN'*s hand, happy as a boy with this testimony.*)
"Moved down this morning!" Why, you're a poet!
(*Turning to others.*)
The perfessor's a poet – and he doesn't know it!
(*Laughs at his own corn and pumps* SEEN'*s hand. No one joins in.*)
Thank you, doctor, thank you perfessor.
You've heard the truth, the truth God bless her.
Two billion years and more this Eden was aborning,
But Eve and I found it only this morning.
Now is there anyone, Soc, Red, or Tory,
Who wants this paradise blown to glory? . . . .
Mr. Powers, he's your witness. Thank *you*, perfessor. (*Sits.*)

POWERS: (*Rising, to* SEEN.) Man-Cain this brief new morning came –
But when a-wither, when away?
O sage Promessor, say.

SEEN: (*Caught offguard by the question, but remaining the honest scientist.*)
Hmmm. Mayhap another thousand generations till
Ice-press return again, tombing the Inlet.

LEGION: Now, now, perfessor, that's only speculation.
Anyway, we'd blast the ice back. Atomic energy.

SEEN: Doubtless man can endure, yet this inlet would drown.

POWERS: Forever endure?

SEEN: (*Cautious.*) Forever? Forever is—long. All suns wane, or swell.

POWERS: And when our sun alters?

SEEN: Then a sleek ball of ice, or of stone boiling.

POWERS: (*Relentlessly.*) And life?

SEEN: Life? Though man leap to Mars, he is lost in this fur:

POWERS: (*Ironic gesture to Hearing.*) You hear, O Hearing?
To blow this vain Man-cover skywards now is to advanquish by a jingle comic second what Adamizing Father Sun desires. Thank you, Prophetic-facer Sane. (*Stalks to blackboard, chalks a small "5" under* LEGION's *total, stalks back and takes seat.*)

PRESIDENT: Any more questions, Mr. Legion?

LEGION: (*Jumps up automatically, but he hasn't any.*) Questions? Uhhh yes. (*Looks at* SEEN *who waits dutifully but deadpan.*) Uhh, no. (*Sits with a sigh and leans head on table – so doesn't see beginning of what follows.*)

PRESIDENT: That will be all, then, Professor Seen, and thank you. (*Gesture to* CLERK, *then begins looking at his notes.*)

CLERK: (*Pops up and routinely begins propelling* SEEN *RIGHT behind* PRESIDENT *towards EXIT RIGHT.*) This way, prof. Please dematerialize this way.

SEEN: (*Allowing himself to be propelled but objecting feebly.*) But dear me, this isn't the way I came in, is it?

MISS TAKE: (*Is preoccupied fixing her hair.*)

PRESIDENT: (*Looking up.*) Wait!

CLERK: (*Already has* SEEN *at exit and is trying to push him into it.*) Please dematerialize this –

LEGION: (*Waking up.*) Hey! He belongs in the ante-room.

PRESIDENT: (*Simultaneously.*) Mr. Clerk! Don't do that! He's still alive!

CLERK: Oops! Sorry, perfessor, sorry. (*Yanking him back and scooting him fast across stage REAR to EXIT LEFT.*) My mistake.

SEEN: (*Still polite, tries to bow to each of the panel as he is being hurried across.*) Thank you. Thank you, gentlemen. Thank you, all. (*Exits.*)

50

PRESIDENT: (*Wiping brow.*) Whew! That was a close one! (*Casts a reproachful eye at* CLERK *who is nipping guiltily back to seat.*) Watch it ... Well now who's next? Mr. Legion I fancy you're ready to try a real ghost again. Shall I suggest – ?

LEGION: (*Jumping up.*) No! thanks, this time I'll pick my own, sir, Someone who really knew this city from away back.

PRESIDENT: You've thought of one?

LEGION: I've thought of one – with your permission –
A Mr. J. C. Deighton, known as Gassy Jack. (*Beams slyly.*)

PRESIDENT: Gassy Jack? ... Wait. You don't mean old Gastown's first barkeep?

LEGION: (*Making it dignified.*) Vancouver's original guest-lodge proprietor --
A *real* old-timer – and a founding-father.

POWERS: A rye and risky choice, Mr. Allegiance.

PRESIDENT: Indeed. You'll have to watch his language, Mr. Legion, we're still on television. However (*Nods to* CLERK.) call him up. Mr. J. C. Deighton, Proprietor, Deighton Arms, 1885.
(LEGION *sits.*)

CLERK: (*Trots over to EXIT RIGHT and calls.*) Mr. J. C. Deighton–Proprietor–Deighton Arms–eighteen—eighty-five please materialize–this—

(*LIGHTS DIM FOR SPOT BUT UP AGAIN QUICKLY.*)

JACK: (*Appears at spot before* CLERK *can finish and rushes out past him towards* PRESIDENT.) Ahoy! At your service, mates –

CLERK: This way, please. (*Scurries to haul* JACK *back just as he is climbing stairs RIGHT to* PRESIDENT'*s rostrum, hand out to* PRESIDENT.) *This way.* (*Propels him behind rostrum to witness box.*)

JACK: (*As he is propelled, looks lingeringly over at* MISS TAKE, *with an ogle.*) And at thee service, lass. (*She registers haughtiness but obviously doesn't mind the attention, even from* JACK). Well gents (*Looking round, as* CLERK *leaves him in witness box and returns to his seat.*), what'll it be? (*Rubbing hands in barkeep's manner.*)

CLERK: You are Mr. J. C. Deighton, proprietor of –

JACK: (*Breaking in.*) Aye, that's me, Gassy Jack, and –

CLERK: of the Deighton Arms, 1882-6, in the settlement of Granville, later incorporated as the city of Vancouver?

JACK: Granville? Vancouver? Coom off it, mate, them's nobs' names. Gastown it was really. Thee knows that. Recorded in Admiralty charts it were, and named after me, Gassy Jack, t'champion talker west o' Hull. 'Twas where Ah was born, in owd England, and a Hull of a place too, if lass here (*Winks at* MISS TAKE.) doant mind an owd sailor what –

PRESIDENT: Now, now, Mr. Deighton, I'm afraid she may, and some of our unseen audience too. Keep it clean if you want to keep materialized.

JACK: (*With a duck to the* PRESIDENT.) O aye, sir, sorry sir, but lor love a dook now all Ah was saying was how Vancouver were really called Gastown and all because a me and so you maun know how it were Ah coom to be called Gassy Jack because –

PRESIDENT: We've all got that point – (LEGION *gets up to examine witness.*)

JACK: – because Ah was born in Hull on a howlin November night, one a them Narth Sea roarers like, so when Ah opened me gob to yell for air I cowt enough sea-wind to toot ma horn the rest av ma natteral life – (*Laughs.*) – oon-natteral life tha might say, havin roon aff to sea afore ma mither could say lor-loomme, and been bosn's mate on –

PRESIDENT: (*Banging gavel.*) Stop! Mr. Legion, take over your witness and – and put a mute in his horn.

LEGION: (*Who has been trying to break in.*) Thank you, sir. And now Jack, this is all very interesting, but time is short. Tell us now, what do you think of old Gastown today?

JACK: (*Beginning subdued but rapidly getting back into swing.*) Today? Eigh, tis a sight now, lad, beant it? Like Hull all over again. Ya know summat? Ya know, when first Ah seed it, twas nobbut a tincan sawmill and a dozen floatshacks? Ah don't know how Ah stook it, me what were woonce a bosn's mate on gert clipper ship, t'owd Invincible she were, no less, and me roamin t'siven soggy seas, but then Ah was –

LEGION: Yes, yes, Jack, but what about now, eh?

JACK: (*From now on, he begins to wander around the Hearing, sometimes to get near various members to emphasize his points, but more often to get close to* MISS TAKE. *From time to time the* PRESIDENT *motions to the* CLERK *who leads* JACK *back to the witness box – though never succeeding in interrupting* JACK's *flow or in keeping him there.*) Eigh, ye've pubs bigger nor icebergs now, lad, but they're as cold to t' spirit, man, and nowt bein droonk but wish-washy cocktails that wouldna get a flea happy, and all like Methody wake wi' nivver a song nor salt-water tale, but take t'owd Deighton Arms now, twas hoob of t'port, ye maught say, and t'loggers opry-house and town the-ayter and if a sailorman wanted t'news or a champion story now there was me, Gassy Jack (*Licks his lips.*), supposin Ah had a soop o' room in me first – (*He's slid over to LEFT steps of rostrum – to* PRESIDENT.) Ye'd nowt be havin a noggin handy for an owd sailorman that –

PRESIDENT: (*Bangs gavel.*) No! (CLERK *hauls him back to witness box.*) This is a courthouse not a saloon. You must stick to the point. Mr. Legion only wants to know if you approve of Vancouver *today.*

JACK: Aye, sorry, capn, but tha knows how tis wi' an owd seadog. Vancouver eh? Today like? Ah tis a gert lubberly place for sure, would ye say? Howso-ivver, Ah'd like it more if they'd nivver changed the name. Waited till Ah'd turned up me toes, they did, them landsharks 'twas, and hearken, twas nobbut a moonth after, the whole kaboodle burned down, ivvery stick a Gastown and the Deighton Arms with it! One a thim landshark's stoomp fires got away, aye twas them gawps again, rattle their teeth, and so tis all new, this – this Vancouver yiv got, and to tell the truth, mates, Ah'd not stick here now, not if Ah were yoong again, and (*He remembers with a sigh.*) alive, nay, tis the Ar'tic Ah'd set me sails for.

Take Aklávik, now, Ah hear t'Eskymoes hev fambly allowances these times, and soop oop their whiskey neat. Happen now t'Mounties wouldna be too watchful on a honest saloon-keeper wi a hoondred sailor's yarns in his yead and –

LEGION: Man, man, if it's money you want, *Vancouver's* where they make it. Don't you realize, Jack, it's a metropolis now – and the point is there are some who don't seem to care if it goes back to the woods and the Indians. You wouldn't like that to happen, would you?

JACK: Eigh, t'would be waste, happen so. (*He is really more occupied with* MISS TAKE *at this moment.*) Though coom to mention Indians, Ah allus had a soft spot for Klootches. Ah'd a kept shipshape if ma owd squaw'd lived, woon Ah got oop Fraser wen Ah was steamboatman dodging bullets –

PRESIDENT: (*Bangs gavel.*) Will the witness answer the question?

JACK: Ah boot Ah am, for ye see twas all of because ma Klootch-lass had forty silver dollars she'd saved – and that's anoother story but a grand woon Ah could tell ye – that we was able to buy three gert barrels a whisky and move to Inlet, and if we'd nivver done that there'd nivver been a Gastown at all, ma jollies, and –

LEGION: *Very* interesting, Jack, but we must get back to –

JACK: Two hogshead with a plank over 'em for a bar, and third barrel on top t'plank, and a belayin pin off owd Invincible for to settle fights. Aye, twas me squaw started Vancouver (*Sighs, slows down, genuinely moved by his memories.*) – but then, mates, she oop and died on me. (*Takes out a bandanna, wipes a tear, then licks his lips.*) Ah could do wi' a tot of whiskey to toast her. (*Looks at* PRESIDENT.) Just from a bit of mumps she coom foul of, capn, and Ah was a stoven man from that day. (*Pauses, but sees* PRESIDENT's *gavel about to descend and rushes on lively again.*) So Ah got me a new squaw, aye a champion young biddy Ah paid t'owd Chief high for her, but, mates, she'd go on tear ivvery full of moon and give out ivvery nobbin of whiskey when Ah was away from saloon – happen, on a bit of spree mysen – and then she'd nip back to Chief's longhouse and Ah'd hev to go fetch her again, and –

LEGION: Jack, please – (*Gives up, sits.*)

JACK: Howsoever she were a round warm Klootch-lass and a worker, aye she were, and if tis all t'same to you gen'mn (*Growing winsome.*) Ah'd be reeght grateful if we called her oop too now, just for a bit like, and (*Wets his lips again.*) let pair of us slip off for tot o' grog soomwheers, that is a coorse when yer all through wi'me here.

PRESIDENT: (*Bangs gavel.*) No! Mr. Deighton, you've been materialized solely to answer questions at this Hearing. Then you go back to – to wherever you came from.

JACK: (*Looking hangdog.*) Aye, aye Capn. Just t'same (*Making wry mouth.*) Ah *would* like a wet of t'whistle. Did I ivver tell ye aboot time Ah was in Callyforny dodgin hordes a grizzlies and greaser bandits and –

PRESIDENT: (*Raises gavel again.*) I've had enough. It's time to dematerialize this –

JACK: Nay, nay, Capn, wait, forgive an owd sailorman, gassy be name, gassy be nature. (*Serious now.*) Happen there besummat Ahm wantin to say, oney Ah can git ma toongue round it – dry as tis. Master Legion here, he's worrit about his city, reet? Aye. But look now, why all t'fuss? Why woory? Gert bludey ports, why, chaps, they're dime a doozen. When sailorman's yoong, port's nobbut a place for gettin drunk and makin loove, and then happen for sailin away from, fast like. And when be he's owd and fair capped wi' sea, he want nowt but a place like own Gastown, place (*He slows because he has them all interested now.*) wi' clean water around it yet, and gert thoompin trees, and deer wandering in at night. . . . Coorse, now Ah'm again destroyin things, even gormless gert cities, Ah'm agin violence an fights – hav ye ivver knowd a saloon-keeper that wasn't? But what Ah'm thinkin you two mought do, Master Legion and Master Powers now, is go fifty-fifty like. Supposin Master Powers lets Master Legion ship out his *real* friends, there'll nowt be many, real chums nivver are, but leastways ship out folks he wants to keep, and settle em up coast, happen, so they'll be startin new places, *little* places – and see that we keep em small this time. Aye, ba goom that's the way. (*Gestures to* POWERS *and* LEGION.) You two fellers splice hands on it. And let rest of t'gormless buggers go down to Davy Jones.

POWERS: O Judgement Day-ton, whom would you sheep from goats?

JACK: Eh?

PRESIDENT: He means whom would you ship out and whom would you leave?

JACK: Ah! Oh, happen Ah'd ship out t'pretty lasses – (*Leers at* MISS TAKE *who bends at once to her note-taking.*) them that'd work spry, that is, and help a chap. Aye, t'sonsy lasses and folks that really laugh and have foon. Noan of rest matter. Ye know, mates, there's a desperit pack of hippycrits in big cities – cardsharpers and shipchandlers, and landsharks like what burned up owd Gastown, and psalm-singin sods, preachers like, Ah nivver gi' mooch for most of t'missionary fellers, and that sets me o'mind of story. You gemmn nivver heard one about missionary and bosun's girl? Seems they was shipwrecked together, see and –

LEGION: Please, Jack, not here –

JACK: (*He is moving slyly towards wrong exit, LEFT.*) And when it coom night-time, like –

MISS TAKE: (*Squeals and covers ears.*)

PRESIDENT: Come away from that ante-room! (*Bangs gavel.*) Clerk, get him!

CLERK: Hey! (*Rushes and grabs* JACK *just as he is about to escape to ante-room.*) You come back here. (*They struggle but* JACK *is too much for him.*) Help! (MISS TAKE *stares with her hands still to her ears,* POWERS *sits unruffled, but both* PRESIDENT *and* LEGION *leap up and join the struggle. They manage to haul* JACK *across stage REAR towards EXIT RIGHT.*)

JACK: Avast, Ah weant go back wi'out nip. . . . Just one! . . .

CLERK: (*Between puffs and struggles.*) Mr. Deighton will you please – dematerialize – this – way.

LIGHTS OUT and SPOT UP on RIGHT EXIT

JACK: (*As he is pushed out.*) Wait! Ye haven't heard rest of ma – stoory. (*Disappears before last word, which is heard from wings.*)

LIGHTS UP

POWERS: (PRESIDENT, LEGION *and* CLERK *return puffing to their seats.*) (*To* LEGION). There goes the very gas your city swelled from. (LEGION *is too disgusted and puffed to try replying.*)

57

EPISODE 6

PRESIDENT: (*Smoothing his ruffled hair and clothes.*) Well, Mr. Legion, I hope you'll pick your next witness with more discretion.

LEGION: Don't worry, I'm through. Through with spooks, through with this whole tomfoolery.

PRESIDENT: Hmmm. Not quite, Mr. Legion. Mr. Powers still has his innings. You have some witnesses to be materialized. Mr. Powers?

POWERS: (*Rising.*) The Offence of the Future, Mr. Precedent, presumpts one whitness from the past, and He'll consent us. With your permission, sir, I'll cull Long Will of Langland.

LEGION: (*Rising.*) Objection. Irrelevant witness.

PRESIDENT: Irrelevant?

LEGION: Never heard of him. (*Sits.*)

POWERS: He lived no less, my learning friend, and with his poet's hand plucked London's pride six sanctuaries agone.

PRESIDENT: Objection over-ruled. He is well known to the Ministry of History. Author of, I believe, *Piers Plowman*?

POWERS: Right, sir.

PRESIDENT: (*To* CLERK.) Have him materialize.

CLERK: (*Goes to EXIT RIGHT, looking confused.*) Long-will-of-land – the author-of-I-believe – (*To* PRESIDENT.) what was that again, sir?

PRESIDENT: (*Patiently.*) Piers Plowman. It's a fourteenth century poem. But "Long Will of Langland" ought to be enough to fetch him.

CLERK: Long Will of Langland – please materialize this way. (*Lights out,* LANGLAND *appears in spot as* CLERK *conducts him centre front.* LANGLAND *crosses himself and bows.*)

LANGLAND: God save you sire, and grace us all.

PRESIDENT: Welcome, Long Will.

> (CLERK *takes* LANGLAND *to witness box and then takes his seat.*)
> (MISS TAKE *shows some awe of* LANGLAND *at first but she soon develops note-taking difficulties with him, gets bored, and goes back to her nails and face.*)

LEGION: (*Rising.*) I must again object, sir, to raking up this witness. How could he know Vancouver? I challenge here his fitness.

POWERS: His spirit walks her streets and straits each day.

LEGION: Bah, a medieval egghead, another of these spooky queers. And the government admits that he's been dead six hundred years.

PRESIDENT: It's my impression, Mr. Legion, that the author of *Piers Plowman* still enjoys a form of life as real as that of, let us say, Mr. J. C. Deighton. Objection overruled. You may proceed, Mr. Powers. (LEGION *sits.*)

POWERS: (*To* LANGLAND.) Tell us, Long While, what see you in Vinecouver? What saw you there this yesterday?

LANGLAND: Yester? Yester in the morning I mused upon a mountain,
Saw the city wake and wink its million windows.
South walked a hoary wood-waste of houses
Massing to the river like lemmings on the march,
Jerry-new cottages jostling jowl to jowl
Down to the fouled and profit-clogged Fraser,
The pile-impaled river plotting its floods.
Then I looked east –

LEGION: (*Up again.*) Mr. President, again I must object.
This is a most unfair account,
A dreary flim-flam full of dialect
And not a word about the things that count.

POWERS: All the bitter for you, Mr. Allegion, when you come to crassexamine.

LEGION: (*Feeling really persecuted, gives* POWERS *a hollow laugh.*)
Ha, ha. All you do is sit and pun,
But I can see this spook is just begun –
Please let *me* get a word in – one!

PRESIDENT: Perhaps, Mr. Powers, you wouldn't mind if Mr. Legion occasionally interrupts this witness with relevant questions?

POWERS: (*Suavely as ever.*) Neither object nor objections.
To the quest or to the questions.

LEGION: Hmph. All right then, just to start with,
Does this witness realize
When he runs down our metropolis
How fast it got to be this size?
Ninety years ago a tent-town,
Rock and bush and stump,
Mud for sidewalks, cows for tractors,
Just a logger's dump.
Now – almost two million people!
And our river, Mr. Long Will,
May be dirty but it's *busy*,
Every hundred yards a mill:
Last year we got another
Billion dollars out of trees.
And there's salmon in that Fraser,
Twenty million bucks from these.
Then there's –

LANGLAND: Yea, all this yammer I hear yet it yieldeth me naught.

LEGION: Yeah, yammer yourself, you – !

PRESIDENT: Please, Mr. Legion! Manners, manners!

LEGION: (*Almost tearful.*) Well, look, he didn't even mention
Our helicopter jetport, or the Plastickville Extension!
(*Sits disgustedly.*)

LANGLAND: Then I looked eastward and saw a legion more
Of harried eyes hurrying down the hills for wages,
Mild folk some, and some merciless, West then I turned my
eyes –

LEGION: (*Up.*) West so soon! Saw you naught in the east!
O damn, now he's got *me* doing it!
Look Mr. Longhair, our workers aren't dejected.
They've got the highest standards in the Universe –
Well, Americans, of course, are always excepted –
And if they couldn't work they'd feel a lot worse.

PRESIDENT: Was that a question, Mr. Legion?

LEGION: Uh? (*Flopping down again.*) No.

POWERS: Please continue, Mr. Longlast. You were about to decry the
waste-ern view.

LANGLAND: Yea there I saw a soft middleclass swaddled in trees,
In unfrequented churches, and in fears not a few.
Chained as fast to profits as poorer folk to wages,
Their roofs and hopes higher but higher still their mortgages.
Some knew nobleness, and neighborly lived:
Some had milk in morning to melt their bellies' ulcers,
And rode alone to office, an ego to an auto.

LEGION: (*Up.*) Mr. Minister, to listen to this witness
I challenge the wisdom –
He's attacking Christianity
And the whole profit system.

POWERS: All the batter for your case, Mr. Legion, if my wetness prove
submersive.

LEGION: But he's talking like a Red – at a Public Hearing!

POWERS: My worldly friend need not be up-armed. Master Langland is
colour-deaf and treats this merely as a Public Seeing. . . . Mr.
Alackland, north now?

LANGLAND: Yea north I gazed last, through a skyfull of grime,
Glimpsed the grizzled harbours and a graveyard of smokestacks,
A wilderness of wires and a weedbed of poles.

LEGION: (*Up again.*) You can't have industry and keep your sky blue!
And our climate's perfect, all the year through. (*Sits.*)

LANGLAND: (*In general he ignores* LEGION.)
Beyond the tamed shores that no tide cleansed
Rose the raped mountains, scarred with fire and finance,
And raddled with the lonely roofs of the rich,
Of barristers and bookies and brokers aplenty
Of agents for septic tanks, for aspirin, or souls.
Executives, crooners, con-men a few –

LEGION: (*Bouncing up.*) Now look – *some* rich are maybe crooked,
But most of them are straight,
And you're talking of the houses
Of folk who really rate,
Homes like Old England's
Or homes of tomorrow –
Whaddya mean they're lonely?
Where's all this sorrow?
Gardens full of roses,
Their own private creeks,
All nestling at the foot
Of the snow-capped peaks.

PRESIDENT: (*Raps gavel.*) We've been very patient, Mr. Legion, but if you
are going to continue interrupting we must insist that you find
more interesting clichés than "snow-capped peaks." . . . Go on,
Mr. Langland. (LEGION *subsides.*)

LANGLAND: Down I strayed then as the sun stood above me,
Trod down Cambie to the tall grey town.
Softly in Powell Street I heard the pimps whisper.
And Cordova was lined with loggers and leggers,
Honest men and reefers, rubadubs and bums –

LEGION: Why I thought the skid-road boys would have been your chums!

LANGLAND: (*Ignores him.*)
I fared then to a harbour where fish-heads floated,
Saw longshoremen sweating and sailors aplenty,
While a shipload of salesmen sailed to a convention
Whiskeyed for the weekend – and their wenches with them.

LEGION: Is that all you saw in the gateway to the Orient?
            What about the world's most majestic liners?
            The yachts? . . . The romantic moonlight cruising?
            And the special trips for the visiting Shriners?

LANGLAND: I sped then to the city's heart, searching for souls,
            But my ears were dinged with dollars and newsies crying doom.
            I saw ward-heelers ride to polls and wangle all the taxes
            And –

LEGION: I wish you'd hang around Seattle for a change!

LANGLAND: Yea, there but here too, I have heard the hearts hopping
            To hope or hate in tune with the headlines,
            Cursing blacks, browns or Jews each week, though blessing
                                    Christ on Sundays.

LEGION: There he goes again, running down religion!

LANGLAND: Came at last in twilight to a tree-tall park
            Where ladies gawked through cage-bars at their naked cousins
            Or bared themselves on beaches that breathed of flesh and
            sewage –

LEGION: (*Up.*) Is this Stanley Park! Really, Mr. Minister,
            The motives of this witness are definitely sinister.
            The picknickers' mecca, the boaters' dream,
            Alpine vistas, and tea with cream!
            Why this is where our cityfolk release all their tensions!
            And even a hellfire preacher might mention
            The coloured fountain in Lost Lagoon or
            The special canoes for the honeymooner!

LANGLAND: Yea but when I moved below the boughs, I marked how the
            lovers
            Must hide from the moon's eye, for love is here illegal
            And laid away in bushes –

LEGION: Ah ha! Free love now!

MISS TAKE: (*Gives a little squeal.*)

LANGLAND: (*Strongly, rising from satire to assertion now.*)
Nay but the love of God is always free, and love of man too,
And if ye lack love, all your living's lifeless,
Love too of truth, and of your children yet to be,
Love of joy and giving joy, and gaining love by loving,
Lust for peace and man's mind and what men can do.
(*He moves out of the box past* LEGION *to FRONT LEFT of table and surveys them all.*)
Yea your folk that walk fat are fallen sick with fear,
Taking but the time's toys and trashing all the future,
Lunatic in laughter, lost in mere getting,
And haunted by a skydoom their own hates have sealed.
(LANGLAND *stalks slowly and silently to CENTRE FRONT and bows to* POWERS.)

POWERS: (*After pause.*) Thank you, Master Will. Your wightness, Mr. Legion. (*Sits.*)

LEGION: (*Rising with gloomy stubbornness but quickly warming.*)
Well all I want to say is, we've got faith in B.C.
Our motto's "We, prosper by Land and by Sea."
We're the Hub of Tomorrow, the Future's Baby,
We're here to stay, and I don't mean maybe.

POWERS: (*Rises.*) Excuse me, Mr. President, but on a point of infamation my louded friend is massinformed. He states Wancouver is the Future's baby, but the Office of the Future nowhen admits paternity. We contend, sir that the past alone is putative.

PRESIDENT: Hmm. The point's well taken. The Clerk will note it. Now, has your witness finished?

LANGLAND: Yea.
POWERS: (*To* LEGION.) Unless my lurid friend would care to Christen him further. (*Sits.*)

LEGION: That one-day tourist? He doesn't know the score. He's a medieval Bolshevik. We've had enough and more. (*Sits.*)

PRESIDENT: Thank you then, Mr. Langland. And good-day. (*Nods to* CLERK.)

CLERK: (*Trots around behind rostrum to get* LANGLAND *but the latter has already stalked over and is already by RIGHT EXIT.*) Please dematerial —
(*LIGHTS DIM. SPOT on* LANGLAND.)

LANGLAND: (*Not waiting for him.*) God's day and God's even, and God save ye all. (*SPOT OUT.* LANGLAND *disappears.*)
(*LIGHTS UP.*)

CLERK: Dematerialize this – (*SHRUGS*). Independent type.
(*Goes back to seat.*)

EPISODE 7

PRESIDENT: Well, gentlemen, no more witnesses? (*Looks at* POWERS *then* LEGION; *both shake heads.*)
Then perhaps we may conclude this Hearing.
Any comments to add, before we do? Mr. Powers?

POWERS: A comma only, to the sentence each witness has pronounced. (*Rising.*) The future contends, sir, no reason has been rhymed why we should not proceed to – damn.

PRESIDENT: (*Coolly.*) Uhhmn. (*Writing.*) Noted. . . . Mr. Legion? Anything to add?

LEGION: (*Rising.*) I certainly have. In the first place –

MRS. A.: (*Walking up aisle of theatre.*) Just a minute, Mr. Legion. (*All members of Hearing, startled, look out to her. She mounts steps to stage.*) And you, Mr. President. (*She walks slowly, determinedly, to FRONT CENTRE and into V-angle of tables.*) This is a Public Hearing, gentlemen?

PRESIDENT: (*Caught off guard.*) What? Er, yes. But-but who are you?

MRS. A.: I am a Public Hearer. I live just two blocks east.

PRESIDENT: But haven't you a TV set, or a radio at least?

MRS. A.: (*Airily surveying the panel.*) I turned it off and came to testify.

PRESIDENT: But-but if you've been listening you'll know the reason why –

MRS. A.: Why I can't be heard? Because I live?
(*Walks over to* POWERS, *who is still standing, as is* LEGION.)
And love? We'll see. You, Mr. Powers,
If you are really Powers, and sit above,
You cannot fear what a mere living housewife says?

POWERS: (*For first time he shows an edge of surprise, even apprehension. Here is the only opponent who can possibly be his match.*) My unpliant clients neither fear nor favour, madam. Stay saying on for all your hours. (*He sits, to register unconcern.*)

MRS. A.: (*Swirls over to* LEGION *who is still standing gaping, not sure if this is friend or foe, and still wanting to get his summation in.*)
And you, Mr. Legion, though I'm no civic V.I.P. that you've invited,
And we have thoughts as far apart as moon and sun,
And though I grant each ill these ghosts today have cited –
(*Strongly.*) Yet gladly do I walk beneath this city's sky,
and will till I'm undone.

LEGION: (*Slow dawn of delight.*) You mean you *like* Vancouver?
(*Makes as if he is going to hug her, but she draws back.*)
At last! Someone to tell the *truth*! (*Takes her arm.*)
Of course we want to have your testimony, lady.
(*Steering her toward WITNESS BOX, he sees* PRESIDENT *with gavel lifted.*) Now, Mr. President, *please* –

PRESIDENT: (*Shrugs, puts gavel down.*) If you wish – but she seems very much alive and her testimony wont stick in the record. Hmm. We'd better have the name anyway.

CLERK: Name, please.

MRS. A.: (*Carelessly.*) My name is anyone's.

MISS TAKE: (*Fed up and wanting to go home.*) How do I spell *that*?

CLERK: N.E. Wuns, I guess. W-U-N-S. Right, miss?

MRS. A.: Any way – but put down "Mrs."

PRESIDENT: Very well, madam – but remember you're off the record.

MRS. A.: (*Steps out of box and makes walking tour of panel FRONT and arrives at* POWERS *by the end of speech.*)
Whether the record mutes me,
Or my child unloose me to sorrow,
Whether the glaciers glide,
Or the sun scream down tomorrow –
I woke today with my husband,
To the bronze clashing of peaks,
To the long shout of the ocean,
And the blood alive in my cheeks.

Though the jetplanes drew their chalk-lines
Over a blackboard sky
The eraser sun undid them,
And a mastering hawk walked high.
Two flickers knocked on a cedar's door,
Three finch ran fugues in the wind,
And the scent of primula moved in my world,
However my world had sinned.

POWERS: (*Rises, smiling.*) O pettafull lady, is this all your shell and shelter
from the blast? The Future hedonizes not these sinsualities, and
though your smile is dew upon a morning web – our snake has
Eved the spider. (*Sits.*)

MRS. A.: And yet I live! Damnation is not *now*;
The hill of Paradise is always passed, and Hell lifts plain,
These twain the sweet hard mountains of our Purgatory
Our will has raised, and will again.

LEGION: (*Puzzled, but still hoping she is on his side, he has followed her
over to* POWERS.) Madam, go on, that's good, don't let *him*
bother you!
If you need help, I'll father you.

MRS. A.: (*Turning on* LEGION *so suddenly he steps back.*)
You father me? No, never!
I am the cool Vancouver's kin, not yours,
And foster daughter to the Headman mild;
In the professor's logic I am woven,
By the rank sailor's flesh my mind is cloven,
And I am yet that priestly plowman's child.
(*She moves RIGHT behind* MISS TAKE *and looks at* PRESIDENT.)
For all mankind is matted so within me
Despair can find no earth-room tall to grow;
My veins run warm, however veers time's weather;
I breathe Perhaps – and May – but never – No.
Under the cool geyser of the dogwood
Time lets me open books and live;
Under the glittering comment of the planets
Life asks, and I am made to give.

POWERS: (*Softly, behind her, remaining seated.*)
Perhappy child, there's still the wrackening.
For every favor fever, for every joy a jar.
Pompeian ladies loved the outlean of Vesuvius!

68

LEGION: (*Rushes around to stand between her and seated* POWERS.)
Now ma'am, don't let him put you off the track.
I'd like to have you tell the Minister
Something about our climate, and our factories,
And all the sights – from Bowen to Westminster!

MRS. A.: (*She pushes him away in the direction of RIGHT EXIT.*) I'm
not your witness! I need your silence only. (*From now on she
unobtrusively blocks any move of* LEGION *to get back to the table,
and gradually crowds him towards EXIT.*)

LEGION: But ma'am your poetry is miles beyond the Prof's.
If you can keep this up and cover all the region
We'll have the Tourist Bureau print a million copies.
They'll never damn us then, or my name isn't Legion!

MRS. A.: (*Putting a hand on each of* LEGION's *shoulders and looking at
him intently.*) Your name *isn't* Legion – mine is.

LEGION: (*Dumbfounded.*) Hey, now, wait a minute, lady, I – (*Laughs
weakly.*)

MRS. A.: (*Pushing him back another step.*) And only in your absence
Can I think to speak.

LEGION: (*Growing alarmed.*) Watch what you're doing!

PRESIDENT: (*Mildly amused.*) Really madam, you're not going to –

MRS. A.: (*Suddenly, with great authority.*) Mr. Pseudo-Legion,
Please dematerialize – this (*Shoving him.*) way.

LEGION: (*Managing to stand, on brink.*) You can't do this to *me*!
(*Waves frantically.*) Mr. President!

MISS TAKE: (*Shrieks.*)

CLERK: (*Jumps up and runs over but only to hover ineffectively.*)

PRESIDENT: O now really, Mrs. Anyone. I'm presiding here.

MRS. A.: (*Firmly blocking the panting* LEGION.)
Presiding, but you cannot interfere.
You're only History . . . Come, Mr. Living Ghost, be gone, be
ghosted.

LEGION: (*Agonized.*) Wait! I still got to summarize my case! . . . I protest,
I –

MRS. A.: (*Takes hands off* LEGION *and makes mesmeric passes at him.*)
Abracadabra!

LIGHTS SLOWLY DIM.

LEGION: I ain't *dead*, it isn't fair, I'm –

MRS. A.: (*Chanting.*)
Pots and pans and Chambers of Commerce,
Roosters, boosters, chisel and cheese-cake –
SHOOO!

LEGION: (*At this moment* CLERK *decides to come in on* MRS. A.*'s side and
gives him a shove.*) – alive! (*Exits with a strangled cry as
LIGHTS OUT.*) I'm a-lie – ! (*LIGHTS UP.*) MRS. A. & CLERK,
*both smiling demurely, come back hand in hand and stand on
the RIGHT of the rostrum, looking up at* PRESIDENT. *He looks
down with official disapproval that slowly changes to a grin as
broad as theirs.*)

PRESIDENT: Well! . . . I must confess I've been wanting to do that myself
for a long time. However (*With some pretence at regaining
control of things.*), it's very irregular conduct on the part of
both of you, and it's high time I closed this Hearing. (*Lifts
gavel.*)

CLERK: Hooray! (*Suddenly releases* MRS. A.*'s hand, vaults to his seat,
and begins gathering up his files slapdash.*)

MRS. A.: (*Shrugs, walks to* POWERS.) Very well, but I've more to say to
Mr. Powers. The rest of you may go if you like. We'll lock up.

MISS TAKE: Oh goody! (*Gaily slips cover on tape-recorder and snaps her
note-pad shut. Gets her compact out.*)

MRS. A.: (*Turning suddenly to* CLERK.) Mr. Clerk, give me the key.

CLERK: (*Scarcely looking up from business of packing away his files, flips key to* MRS. A.) O.K. Ma'am. . . . Catch!

MRS. A.: Ooops. . . . . Got it.

PRESIDENT: Now, now, not *quite* so fast. . . . First, I must declare the Hearing ended, you know. . . . Well, then, it's ended. (*Bustle of* MISS TAKE *and* CLERK.) But wait, there's my judgement! . . . Judgement is (*He looks at* POWERS, *as if for a cue, but* POWERS *turns from him to look at* MRS. A.) – of course – (*All are stock still.*) –

POWERS: (*Still staring at* MRS. A. *and speaking as if compelled.*) Suspended!

PRESIDENT: Errr . . . yes . . . of course . . . suspended. Hmmm. Mr. Clerk, you can shut off the television.

CLERK: (*With his new-found gaiety.*) Righto! (*Waltzes over, clicks it off, returns.*)

MISS TAKE: May I go now, sir? (*Jumping up and patting her dress.*)

PRESIDENT: Er, yes. I suppose we'd all better be going. Drat it, where's that gavel?

CLERK: (*In growing holiday mood.*) Just leave it, sir, I'll come back tomorrow and pick it up with my files and this junk of Mr. Legion's.

MISS TAKE: (*Tripping off RIGHT.*) Nightie-nightie everybody.

CLERK: Hey! Not that way! (*Grabs her from dumbly walking out the dematerializing EXIT.*) This way.

MISS TAKE: Oooh. Thanks!

CLERK: (*Not letting go, steering her toward LEFT EXIT.*) You need somebody to see you home. Somebody like me. . . . Goodnight, everybody else.

PRESIDENT: Here, you two, wait for me. We've got a job on our hands. (*They stop.*) Yes. A report to the Missing Persons Bureau. Immediate. On Mr. Legion

CLERK: O Lord yes. (*Rushes back to his files, grabs papers.*) I'd forgotten him already. In milluplicate!

PRESIDENT: (*Rises, steps down LEFT from rostrum.*) Coming, Mr. Powers?

POWERS: (*Without taking eyes off* MRS. A.) Coming but nowhere gone. I stay enchantressed by our leading lady.

PRESIDENT: Well, it's your Private Hearing now, and no records taken. (*Joins* CLERK *and* MISS TAKE.)

CLERK: Night, ma'am. Don't forget to lock up. (MRS. A. *smiles at him. He takes long look at* POWERS.) Gad naught, Mr. Pow-wowers. (*Exits fast, with* MISS TAKE.)

PRESIDENT: Goodnight, madam. (*Bows.*) Night, Mr. Powers. Judgement reserved – *sine die* – eh?

MRS. A.: (*Cheerfully.*) Goodnight, Mr. Minister.

POWERS: (*As* PRESIDENT *exits.*) God's night, Mr. Moonister, and a good waning. (*Turns to her.*) Madoom, my compliments. (*Bows.*) You guessed these ghost-men out. . . . And now?

MRS. A.: (*Walks past him and mounts* PRESIDENT's *rostrum, sits.*) Now you.

POWERS: Me? (*Laughs, slowly mounts rostrum and stands behind her chair.*) I'm all-wise just behind your reach, and yet (*Reaching arms around her waist.*) – I hold you.

MRS. A.: (*Smiles and without effort parts his hands and looks up at him.*) But ever I am loosed by hope.

POWERS: (*Moves around on rostrum to stand on RIGHT of her, arms folded.*) And lost, in this unhopey world.

MRS. A.: (*Looking straight out, chin up.*) No. My mind's unconquered.

POWERS: Men conquer their own minds, and canker others'.

MRS. A.: By all the past we know our freedom is renewable each moment.

POWERS: (*Takes her hand.*) By all your Past the Future has
                              condoomed you.
        (*Pulls her slowly up.*)
        Prepare to follow Legion (*He gestures towards EXIT RIGHT.*)
                              to the ghosts.

MRS. A.: No! (*Pulls him easily back so that he has to sit in the* PRESIDENT'S
        seat now.) Never! (*She stands over him.*)
        I am mistress over you, my master Power.
        The only future's what I make each hour.

POWERS: (*Looking sardonically out and up.*)
        Hours that hasten to the sun's sahara.

MRS. A.: (*Looking in the same direction.*)
        Till sun sears we make him sire us.
        Till then all shapes and sounds will fire us,
        Our thinkers knit them and our artists net.

POWERS: (*Rises, stands facing her across the chair.*)
        Think you in these to find the Headman's peace?
        That bard of paradays is plucked
        And all his comeforth gone beyond Vancovery.
        Your world is armagadding;
        No conjury of little folk undoes its warlocks.
        You're now too billion many.

MRS. A.: The more to want and thus to will – and then we've caught it.
        How many leaps of light away peace spins
        The heart builds its long telescope to plot it.

POWERS: But what is peace, if all the earth's a gassy jacktown?

MRS. A.: It still has its becoming.
        There's not a day that kindness does not rise
        Like grass through every pavement's crack.

POWERS: (*Jeeringly.*) What? Through every Mastered Longwill strait?

MRS. A.: His eyes were on the sins he loved to hate.
He heard the bomb but not the children whistling.
Yet children, grown, may sing a doom awry.
He did not stay to see the selfless deeds that multiply
And hum like simmering bees across my city's gardens,
Storing for winter all that summer pardons.

POWERS: (*Moving to tower close over her.*)
But lady, lady, I threaten ever-the-lease.

MRS. A.: (*With a head-toss.*)
How could I know, without the threat of death, I lived?

POWERS: But do you know why you defy me?

MRS. A.: (*Looking up almost tenderly at him.*)
That you might also be.
Without my longer will, my stubborn boon,
You'd have no mate to check with but the cornered moon.
(*Slowly*) It's my defiant fear keeps green this whirling world.

POWERS: (*With a gesture of checkmate.*) Brave-O, my wise mad-madam.
(*Steps down RIGHT and reaches up his hand to her.*) Come . . .
(*She puts her hand in his.*) We'll lock away . . . and mate again
(*She jumps down beside him.*) . . . on Judgement Day.

MRS. A.: (*Begins moving with him LEFT around back of rostrum. Their
shadows loom large on the back curtain, his at first much larger,
then gradually shrinking as hers outsizes his.*)
Content – but (*Twirling key.*) I shall keep the Key.

POWERS: (*His arm is around her and he is looking at her with a mixture
of admiration and pity.*)
Content – I'll have the skeleton. (*Measures her with his eyes.*)

MRS. A.: (*They walk to EXIT LEFT,* POWERS *leading. He exits, but she
turns full face to audience.*)
And I – a life. (*EXIT*)

CURTAIN

Vancouver 1952-1957

Appendix

SUGGESTIONS FOR CASTING, MAKE-UP, &
CHARACTER INTERPRETATION.

President of Hearing

A run-of-the-mill provincial politician. For most of the play he is the titular boss and exercises his authority with good temper, sophistication, and a correct show of impartiality. However, he knows that his government has called the Hearing simply to let off public steam, that Mr. Powers is the real power in the government, and so, whatever is said, he will be expected to decide in favor of Powers and the damning of Vancouver. Consequently he is at times bored, at times cynical, with Legion. When Powers surprisingly has to face a real enemy, Mrs. Anyone, the President slides away with sardonic aplomb and recognition of his own inconsequence.

He is the only major character who speaks almost entirely in normal prose, and he should have a prose voice and a prose look. Dress conservative, no trappings except perhaps an academic gown.

Clerk of the hearing

Can be any age or size, a fussy nondescript fellow, soaked in officialese and routine, but capable of boyish revolt under the influence of Mrs. Anyone. His voice is singsong, his dress ordinary.

P.S. Legion.

Preferably young, plumpish, with the red cheeks of high blood pressure, and an out-thrust confident jaw. He should be in marked physical contrast to Powers, his voice high and shrill. He is a man-of-the-peepul, a Chamber of Commerce booster, and a fairly smart lawyer in normal circumstances. But he is knocked off his materialistic base at the start by the curious nature of the Hearing, and grows increasingly frustrated.

He speaks verse, not poetry; his lines are deliberate doggerel and can be rhythmically clowned-up for stylization, if production allows.

Dress: give him a bright tie and a flower in his buttonhole.

Gabriel Powers.

Preferably tall, imposing, not too thin (he must not be a physical duplicate of Langland). He represents both the Death Force and the enigmatic Future and should be dressed to symbolize both, in close-fitting black one-piece jacket and tights, and a hood to match. A faint hint of rib and limb-bone patterns should be sketched on to his suit with luminous white or silver paint. There should, however, be a Buck Rogers touch or two to his suiting, not merely a skeletal one.

His voice is deep and dark-brown, but very clear (to handle the portmanteau words). In contrast to Legion, he speaks a sort of poetry, not doggerel, but it is poetry with very free rhythms.

He talks always out of special knowledge, since he knows what is going to happen, and his tones are tinged with a Hardyean irony, in consequence—with brooding pity for the innocent, and jaunty contempt for Mr. Legion. Only in the play's last lines, when his Death Force meets the Life Force of Mrs. Anyone, does he become completely human and falter in his omniscience and in his terrible quiet confidence.

Miss Take.

An ornamental stenographer with a cute voice.

Capt. Vancouver.

An eighteenth century Englishman with some education and polish but with a touch of sailor-adventurer bluffness. His attitude is polite, a little puzzled, intellectually interested, emotionally indifferent.

His speech should be clipped, with some eighteenth-century pronunciations which sound a bit Irish today. He should pronounce the following words somewhat in this way:

servant	sarvant
earliest	arliest
my orders	me arders.
northwest	narwest

discerned	dissarned
point	pint
girls	garls
sort	sart
Burrard	(with accent on first syllable)

He tends to chop his final g's.

He should be dressed in a half-moon tricorn hat with gold lacing, a brass-buttoned large navy-blue coat, white breeches and leather boots. He should wear a peruque adorned with a white ribbon.

Skuh-wath—etc.

Old, dignified, but capable both of a wry pithy humour and of passion, which should save him from being merely The Noble Redskin. In general he simply witnesses relentlessly to the truth as he remembers it. His anger grows with Legion's crass prodding but it is anger which turns to a kind of nostalgic special-pleading.

Long grey or white hair streams from his shoulders. If accuracy is desired, the hair should be oiled and given a top dusting of eagle down (chicken down will do), as a symbol that he has come in peace. He should wear either an ankle-length cloak of sewn skins (otter was what he had) or a shorter cloak of woven goat's wool. It should be clasped by a huge bone pin. He wears hand-sewn pants of rough wool and high laced moccasins. Squirrel-tail tassels dangle from the shoulders of his cloak.

He can carry a ceremonial stick or rattle of carved cedar.

His speech is guttural, ruminative. He pronounces his name the best way the actor can. Some other words to watch are:

Salish	*say*-lish
Kwakiutl	*quack*-ee-ootl
Sechelt	*see*shelt
salal	sa-*lal*

His face should be painted—the nose to simulate the short sharp beak of an owl (his totem), wide black circles around the eyes, the cheeks grey-white.

Dr. E. O. Seen.

A single-minded cove intent only on saying his piece as an

"expert witness". He can work up enthusiasm about the past, on the basis of scientific evidence, but he is unexcited by the philosophic implications of his own material—implications which Powers of course forces the rest to see.

Perhaps middle-aged, with slightly abstracted air, but not the stage professor please. Decent suit but not new, with leather elbow patches on sleeves.

Since this is "five years from now", and a time of poised doom, he could carry a haversack labelled "EMERGENCY RATION KIT" and a box labelled "GEIGER".

His lines are in Old English metre but the actor should not worry about the metrical form. He is a careful honest professor somewhat under the spell of his own cryptic notes and with a tendency, when he does elaborate, to fall into oldfashioned rhetoric. He loves his subject.

J.C. Deighton.

An historical character, former windjammer and gold prospector, now (at the age of his death) a middle-aged boozy saloonkeep. He is intended to have the charm of the mild psychopath whose gabbiness is based on genuine adventures in his more youthful and less alcoholic days.

No portraits of him have survived. I think of him as short, sturdy, with a small pot, a bit of grog-blossom on the nose, purple cheeks, and a walrus moustache. Blacken out some of his teeth and dress him in the style of the Pacific coast saloonkeeper of the 1880's; shirt-sleeved, without tie, gaudy beer-spotted waistcoat and heavy gold watch-chain, shapeless pants, brown or black derby.

He speaks with a slight Yorkshire accent, since he came from Hull, but his vocabulary is basically a sailorman's. He's a long-playing record and goes at a good clip, cheery and wheezy and always hoping for the drink he never gets. His prose develops its own folk-rhythms.

William Langland.

Fourteenth-century visionary poet and popular reformer, a sort of Catholic Puritan. An old man, gaunt, as tall and thin as possible. Long straggling hair and wild full beard. Let the make-up bring out his flaming damnation eyes.

Though he is a relentless moralizing Jeremiah, he has his mood-shifts. When he speaks of the honest poor, of the innocent, of children, there is momentary pity and tenderness. At other times he is scornful, biting; at others a dogged moralizing cataloguer of the world's sins. But he rises through denunciation to a final positive assertion of Christian charity and love. This theme will sound out of character if the actor has not taken every opportunity to bring out his earlier moments of mournful pity of the human mass.

He speaks with masculine strength, in his own alliterative line. But if the actor gives the lines their normal speech emphases, the verse-rhythms will look after themselves.

Mrs. Anyone.

In her late twenties, a healthy desirable woman, not a brittle Noel Coward type on the one hand or the Great American Mom on the other. As a representative of the Life Force, she can be buxom or not, but she must be lyrical. Her logic may be dubious, her confidence blind, but she has the job of turning the play from damnation to assertion, to belief in the possibilities of life, in the potential ability of Man to triumph over himself even at this late moment. So let's have her shrewd and not shrewish, with lots of supple strength, and the capacity to flirt even with that old Death-Man Gabriel Powers himself. Dress her like a housewife five years from now, however that will be.